Just Add Mistletoe

Addison Moore

Edited by Paige Maroney Smith
Cover Design: Gaffey Media
Published by Hollis Thatcher Press, Ltd.

Books by Addison Moore

Cozy Mystery
Cutie Pies and Deadly Lies (Murder in the Mix 1)
Pumpkin Spice Sacrifice (Murder in the Mix 2)
Bobbing for Bodies (Murder in the Mix 3)
Gingerbread and Deadly Dread (Murder in the Mix 4)

Mystery
Little Girl Lost

Romance
Just add Mistletoe

3:AM Kisses (3:AM Kisses 1)
Winter Kisses (3:AM Kisses 2)
Sugar Kisses (3:AM Kisses 3)
Whiskey Kisses (3:AM Kisses 4)
Rock Candy Kisses (3:AM Kisses 5)
Velvet Kisses (3:AM Kisses 6
Wild Kisses (3:AM Kisses 7)
Country Kisses (3:AM Kisses 8)
Forbidden Kisses (3:AM Kisses 9)
Dirty Kisses (3:AM Kisses 10)

Stolen Kisses (3:AM Kisses 11)

Lucky Kisses (3:AM Kisses 12)

Tender Kisses (A 3:AM Kisses Novella)

Revenge Kisses (3:AM Kisses 14)

Red Hot Kisses (3:AM Kisses 15)

Reckless Kisses (3:AM Kisses 16)

Hot Honey Kisses (3:AM Kisses 17)

The Social Experiment (The Social Experiment 1)

Bitter Exes (The Social Experiment 2)

Chemical Attraction (The Social Experiment 3)

Low Down and Dirty (Low Down & Dirty 1)

Dirty Disaster (Low Down & Dirty 2)

Dirty Deeds Low (Down & Dirty 3)

Naughty by Nature

Beautiful Oblivion (Lake Loveless 1)

Beautiful Illusions (Lake Loveless 2)

Beautiful Elixir (Lake Loveless 3)

Beautiful Deception (Lake Loveless 4)

Someone to Love (Someone to Love 1)

Someone Like You (Someone to Love 2)

Someone For Me (Someone to Love 3)

Burning Through Gravity (Burning Through Gravity 1)
A Thousand Starry Nights (Burning Through Gravity 2)
Fire in an Amber Sky (Burning Through Gravity 3)

The Solitude of Passion

Celestra Forever After (Celestra Forever After 1)
The Dragon and the Rose (Celestra Forever After 2)
The Serpentine Butterfly (Celestra Forever After 3)
Crown of Ashes (Celestra Forever After 4)
Throne of Fire (Celestra Forever After 5)

Perfect Love (A Celestra Novella)

Young Adult Romance
Ethereal (Celestra Series Book 1)
Tremble (Celestra Series Book 2)
Burn (Celestra Series Book 3)
Wicked (Celestra Series Book 4)
Vex (Celestra Series Book 5)
Expel (Celestra Series Book 6)
Toxic Part One (Celestra Series Book 7)
Toxic Part Two (Celestra Series Book 8)

Elysian (Celestra Series Book 9)

Ethereal Knights (Celestra Knights)

Season of the Witch (A Celestra Novella)

Ephemeral (The Countenance Trilogy 1)

Evanescent (The Countenance Trilogy 2)

Entropy (The Countenance Trilogy 3)

Melt With You (A Totally '80s Romance)

Tainted Love (A Totally '80s Romance 2)

Hold Me Now (A Totally '80s Romance 3)

1

Gingerbread Men

Missy

"We'd each like a cup of your minty mountain cocoa and a couple dozen of those fudgy things in the corner." Sabrina Jarrett flicks a perfectly red polished fingernail at the Gingerbread Bakery and Café's famous fudgies. The *we* she is referencing is the two dozen of her closest friends she runs a book club with. "And don't you dare try to push off the disgusting ones with rum in them on me. You know I can't stand the taste of rum, and I am well aware of the fact you did so on purpose the last time." She bats those long, unnaturally extended lashes my way.

Sabrina Jarrett has been a thorn in my side for as long as I can remember. Growing up, it was always Sabrina playing the part of mean girl all the way through high school.

We ended our scholastic careers together at Gingerbread High on the same cheer team. Sabrina was the captain, and she's never let me forget it. And after that, we thankfully went our separate scholastic ways—me away to college in Arizona and her to a university in Oklahoma. But as fate and my poor luck would have it, we've both landed back in Gingerbread. Me with my very own bakery that I co-own with my sister, Holly—and Sabrina as an up-and-coming socialite. Only too bad for Sabrina, Gingerbread, Colorado is the last place on the planet with a socialite circuit.

She turns to leave, then spins back on her spiked stilettos. Sabrina is the only one I know who would brave stilettos after a two-foot snowfall. Her hair is as crimson as her wool coat, and her lips are glossed to match. She looks festive in a caustic way, which pretty much describes Sabrina all of the time.

She wrinkles her nose at the selections in the pastry window. "You'd better throw in some of those red velvet cupcakes. The ones with the mistletoe and bows." She leans over the counter as if she's about to spill a juicy secret and, believe you me, she's more than able. If Sabrina has achieved anything since dropping out of college—she was four units shy of earning her bachelor's in English, *four!*—but I digress, Sabrina has effortlessly achieved the coveted title of town gossip.

I shoot a quick look to Holly, and that expression on her face is mirroring my urge to both scream and cry.

"About how many cupcakes?" I try my hardest not to scowl at the she-devil that has no problem exhausting my inventory. Sabrina is famous for freeloading off the bakery ever since we've opened. I'm half-moved to tell her that the sign on the door doesn't read *Your Personal Pantry*.

"We'll need thirty." Her bright green eyes widen a moment. "The book we're going over this afternoon was rife with heat." She pretends to fan herself and gives a little wink. "You're not seeing anyone, are you, Missy? Maybe I should lend you my copy." She cackles, and shockingly, Holly cackles right along with her.

My mouth falls open as I take a moment to stomp on Holly's toes. Traitor.

"*What?*" My sister bounces away. "It was funny."

I look back to Sabrina in all her glossy magazine glory. She has always reminded me of a magazine pictorial come to life. "I'll tally that up for you in just a moment." I bite the inside of my cheek because I know what comes next in this commerce version of cat and mouse.

Sabrina wags a finger. "Oh, please, don't do that. I've begged and I've begged Daddy not to increase your rent. And by twenty percent?" Her penciled in brows skyrocket into her unwrinkled forehead. It's a well-known fact there are parts of Sabrina's face that simply will not move. Holly says it's because she's full of Botox. I suggested she was full of something else. "How will you ever survive?" Her nails graze over her chest, rife with her false concern. "Consider it tit for tat. And, believe me, you are winning in this deal." She reaches over and steals a cookie off the tray I was busy assembling before she appeared before me like a poltergeist. It's our busiest season of the year, and on top of all of the other madness, I've got the auction at the community center to prepare for. I certainly don't have time for Sabrina Jarrett and her empty threats—or her real ones. If I could decipher one from the other, life might be a little simpler.

"I'll get those treats and cocoa to your table right away."

She turns on her heels before taking a quick step back. "Rumor has it, you're still the best matchmaker this side of the Rockies. If you ever come across a young, hot, stud—don't keep him for yourself." She flashes a contrived smile. "We'd hate to bore the poor man to death. Send him *my* way." She tosses her scarf over her shoulder as she makes her way to the indoor patio where four tables of cackling women run out the real customers with their incessant laughter.

"She conjoined four tables for her book club. No wonder we have no customers. They have nowhere to sit."

"She's terrible." Holly helps gather the fudgies and the cupcakes while I get straight to draining the last of my minty mountain cocoa.

"You didn't think she was so terrible a moment ago." I shoot Holly a look for colluding with the enemy if only for a brief moment.

"Oh, you." She's quick to wave me off, and is she laughing again? She shakes out her sandy blonde hair with a laugh, her periwinkle eyes sparkling in the light. That's what our mother gifted us as far as genetics go—her sandy blonde hair and peculiar shade of eyes. My father and brother wear a dark cap of hair and coffee-colored eyes to match. We've heard a million people say my sister and I are clones of our mother. They say all Winters girls look alike. And it's pretty much true. Holly and her husband, Tom, have a seven-year-old daughter, Savanah, and she swims in the Winters women's gene pool as well. "She's right, though. You do have quite the reputation for being the best matchmaker in the area. Don't you think it's time you find a match for yourself?"

"Are you kidding? I have no time to date. I'm too busy baking yummy treats for Sabrina and her cohorts," I huff as I trickle out the last of the minty mountain cocoa.

I glance to the back and sigh as I spot the two towering gingerbread dollhouses that are currently occupying all of my time and most of my workspace. I'm making one for Mayor Todd's twin daughters. He had the idea that if I made him one he'd showcase it at city hall with a sign that lets everyone know there will be one just like it available at the auction Christmas Eve. Every year, Gingerbread hosts an auction on

Christmas Eve. It's sort of a long-standing tradition to get everyone in our tight-knit community together for such a special holiday. Christmas Day is usually reserved for the family. That way the town sort of gets to celebrate the occasion as an extended family the day before. For as long as I can remember, it's been held at the community center. Everyone dons their finest clothes, there's a potluck, and dancing, and for the last few years, Holly and I have happily provided the desserts. The city actually pays us for our goodies, which is refreshing since Sabrina and her faux socialites have become our unwanted charity effort.

The bells on the front door chime as my mother breezes into the bakery in a flurry.

Before I even bother with a greeting, I call to Jenna in the back to help make all of Sabrina's chocolatey, cocoa, red velvet wishes come true. Jenna works tirelessly for Holly and me, along with a small baking army we've accrued over the last year. Prior to that, Holly and I were running ourselves ragged and almost closed the bakery for good in an effort to hold onto our sanity.

"I'm on it!" Jenna swoops in, and both Holly and I migrate to the end of the counter as I greet my mother with her favorite, a raspberry Linzer bar. Her creamy blonde hair cascades in soft curls down her shoulders. She looks far more like a sister rather than our mother, and I can only hope when I'm her age I look half as amazing.

"You always know how to save me, Missy." She takes a bite and groans with approval. "Now, I have to run to Cater to show a brand new listing—an entire condo complex has landed in my hands! Can you believe it?" Her violet eyes grow twice their size. At fifty-seven, my mother doesn't have a wrinkle to show for it. In fact, she outright glows from within. For years, people have plied her with compliments and then tried to shake her down for her secret, to which she kindly replies, "The fountain of youth lies in the coffee found only at the Gingerbread Bakery and Café." She's forever trying to help drum up business for Holly and me. Mom knows all about business. In the last five years, she's entered into the wonderful world of real estate and is doing quite well for herself. She and Dad own the lumber mill, so she was fortunate enough to stay home while we were little, but after we flew the nest, she got angsty and found her niche in real estate. My brother, Nick, runs the tree lot for the family this time of year, but he's full-time at the lumber mill as well.

"Cater?" Holly makes a face. "That's a half hour away. There's another storm moving in, you know."

Mom makes a face right back. "It's just a quick orientation to the building. I've hired a photographer to meet me there. I'm going to have a few of the units staged before I show it. I'm going big with this one." She does an odd little tap dance as she giggles with glee. It doesn't take much to get my mother giddy. "I'll be back in plenty of time to pick up

Savanah from school. You know she's my top priority." She leans toward Holly with that *I'm about to school you* look on her face. "You know, by the time I was your age, I had all three of you running circles around me."

"*Ugh!*" Holly lifts her hands to her ears. She's about had it with the whole procreation dissertation my mother likes to dole out regularly. "I tell you what. As soon as Tom and I decide to add another child to the family, you'll be the first to know."

Mom gives a silent applause, squealing away with unmitigated glee. Really, it's embarrassing to witness.

She spins back to me as her expression changes on a dime. "Oh, Missy, I need a quick favor! I've got a client meeting me at the office in five minutes, and I really can't stress enough how much I need you to cover. I just can't reschedule the meeting in Cater." Her eyes plead with me all on their own, and I have never been able to say no to my mother. And sadly, she knows it. She's been known to wield this knowledge to her benefit each and every time. I've covered for her so much at the realty office that I feel like an honorary realtor myself.

"Okay, but just this once until after Christmas. I've got a million gingerbread houses on order." It's true. A million and one to be exact. People come as far as Denver to purchase a gingerbread house from Gingerbread. It's as if the town name lends to the credibility of the delectable, sturdy, yet seldom noshed upon dessert.

"Great," she trills just as Holly gifts her a large cup of coffee to go. "I'll see you girls later. Holly, hold down the fort. Mistletoe Winters, comb your hair and slick some gloss on your lips. Rumor has it, you're about to meet an out-of-towner with a dashing smile and a big fat wallet. At twenty-six, you're not getting any younger." She gives a little wave as she heads for the door. "*Toodles!*"

"Toodles," Holly and I shoot back without the proper enthusiasm.

Holly smirks my way. "You think it's a setup?"

"Are you kidding? When has our mother missed an opportunity to set me up?"

I glance at myself in the mirrored wall behind my sister. My nose has a dot of flour on it, and my hair looks as if I've just jogged around the frozen lake at the end of town.

"That looks about right," I mumble as I head for the door.

"*Hey!*" Holly calls after me. "Aren't you going to comb your hair?"

"Mr. Right won't care what I look like on the outside, Holly. It'll be my quick wit and fudgies I snag him with!" I laugh as I hit the frozen tundra right outside the bakery.

Whoever is waiting for me at that realty office isn't getting anywhere near my fudgies.

There is nothing like spending the holiday season in a cozy little town like Gingerbread. The clouds above are filled with their wintery wrath, and the snow on the ground sits fluffy and white, strewn across the entire expanse of Main Street as if someone set out a heavenly white blanket. The shops that line either side of the street are each festooned with wreaths swathed in large red bows. Garland and twinkle lights fill all the shop windows, and there is even a large life-sized Santa standing on the corner where tourists and locals alike stop to take a picture with the plastic man in the red suit. But the real magic happens at night. A couple of years ago, Mayor Todd had the expanse over all of Main Street laced with white lights, and it adds a fairy-tale appeal that makes our small town feel downright enchanting. It's perfectly romantic, and I suppose that's why the romantic in me has truly blossomed. This last year alone, I played an intricate part in pairing six different couples together. *Six*! That's a record, even for me. Two of which are engaged. Molly and Richard have their wedding slated for June, and Tova and Mark have their sights set on Halloween night because they're unconventional that way. I guess you can say I have an eye for all things heart-shaped, and I certainly am great at reading people. I pretty much know right off the bat who a person would be best suited with. And even though she'll deny it to her dying day, it was me that paired Holly with Tom all those eons ago. I knew the second he said he was partial to Italian food, but not necessarily cheese, that only a person equally as quirky could respond well to that. Case in point, Holly has a dairy allergy and yet loves pasta Bolognese. Match made in marinara heaven.

I pause a moment as I scowl at the window of the Knit Wit, the knitting shop that Samantha Holiday owns along with Caroline Lindy. Samantha is more or less a silent partner. It's Caroline who operates as boots on the ground any given day. But neither Samantha nor Caroline is the reason I'm scowling at it. I can't help it. Every time I look that way, it reminds me of another *knit wit*, Graham Holiday, Samantha's son. Graham and my brother, Nick, were best friends growing up, and they spent a vast majority of the time tormenting my sister and me. *Boys will be boys*, my mother used to say. I try to shake all thoughts of Graham right out of my head. *Think about someone too long and they're liable to materialize right before you.* That's another thing my mother used to say.

I quickly come upon Mountain Realty at the end of the street and bustle my way through the egregiously heavy glass door. It's a wonder they have customers at all with that unfriendly fifty-pound greeting. I give a casual wave to Debbie, the receptionist, who currently has the phone cradled to her cheek, her fingers busy gliding across her keyboard. The Mountain Realty office isn't all that big, with just six micro offices set inside the tiny box-shaped building. But in its defense, the inside has recently been remodeled with slate gray vinyl flooring and a mirrored coffee table set in the entry. The scent of fresh paint still clings in the air, and everything about the marble desktops and oversized leather office chairs screams new, new, *new*! I stride by a few of the realtors' offices—Jim, my mother's mentor, whom I can tell is playing a video game on his laptop from the reflection upon the window behind him—something to do with a spacecraft. And there's Gail Diamond, my mother's only real competition in getting that coveted realtor of the year title. Mom told me so herself last week, and to hear her lay it all out, you can tell there is some bad blood brewing under this roof.

I hit the last office, my mother's, and stop in my tracks when I spot a man with broad shoulders, a dark head of hair tilted down as he scrolls through his phone. My stomach does that totally adolescent roller coaster thing that I've grown to despise over the years. Where does my body get off commandeering my emotions without my permission? I never did think it was fair.

I clear my throat as I stride right past him and take a seat. Just as I'm about to welcome him to Mountain Realty—*where dreams are only a sold sign away!*—I stop cold. My muscles freeze solid, and I can't seem to take my next breath.

"Oh, it's just you." I sag as I stare out at the Adonis before me. Yes, it's true. Graham Holiday is every bit the ovary popping god who stepped down from Mount Olympus to dwell with us mortals. But he's also my brother, Nick's, lifelong best friend who just like my brother imposed enough sisterly torment my way I can't help but glare at him a little. Graham may be gorgeous, but he full well knows it. That's the worst trait by far in a human being if you ask me. Okay, so maybe it's not *the* worst, but it sure does head the top of the list.

His bright blue eyes widen with surprise, and that dimpled grin of his beams my way without hesitation.

"Mistletoe Winters." He holds out his arms a moment, and just as easy as that smile glided over his face, it glides right back off. "Wow, you've really grown up."

"Yes, well, a decade will do that to a person."

His dimples press in, and just witnessing the sight gives my stomach that blissful free-fall feeling once again. I really do hate biology right about now.

"It hasn't been a decade." He frowns a moment as he scours my features. "You are beautiful," he whispers, and my mouth falls open, incredulous as if my so-called beauty were the last thing he expected.

"Pardon me? I'm here as a professional, and I'm assuming you came seeking my mother's services. I'm her temp, so I'll have you treat me with a little more respect than you're used to."

"I just meant I hadn't been in New York that long." Graham has lived in New York City for what feels like an eternity, although I'll be the last to admit it. He just so happens to be a high-powered realtor himself.

"So, what are you doing here?" I straighten the piles of paperwork over my mother's desk just to keep my hands busy. My fingers have a panache to want to wrap themselves around Graham's neck whenever possible. There is no one else on record who can push my buttons the way Graham used to. Well, maybe Sabrina. "Let me guess, you're here to steal the Mountain Realty playbook in order to sharpen your game? Need a few hints from my mother, big boy? Manhattan real estate must be really rough."

"*Ha!*" he barks out a laugh so loud the windows rattle. "I'm not here to steal any secrets, I promise. Maybe a few hearts." He gives a little wink, and my insides flip-flop.

"Well, you're not stealing this one. Trust me, I'm keeping the old ticker under lock and key. How long are you in town for?" My finger wraps itself around one of my ashen curls over and over like some biological reflex.

"Around a month." He leans in, and the scent of his spiced cologne warms me. I can't help but note how that deep navy jacket really sets off the cobalt color of his eyes. And how relaxed and outdoorsy he looks in those inky jeans and beat-up boots as if he's trying to convince all of Gingerbread that he's just one of us hardworking folk, not some high society, running in the big leagues city player. Nick has regaled me with one too many *you should see what Graham is doing now* stories. Little does good old Graham know that I'm on the inside track as far as his astronomical sales, the unbelievable models he's mass dating, and let's not forget the penthouse with a spectacular view of Central Park. I'll admit, there was a spark of jealousy in me over his ritzy lifestyle a time or two.

"A month?" I balk. "It must be nice to have retired early. I don't know too many people who can take an entire month off work and still keep a roof over their heads."

A dark chuckle comes from him, and he looks that much more comely. Graham's good looks have never played fair. "I'm here on business. Sort of. Tanner called a family meeting regarding Holiday Pies. I figured why not spend Christmas in Gingerbread. But I need to be on that next plane out day after Christmas. Duty calls, and it's not in Gingerbread."

"All this way for a family meeting?" I'm shocked to hear this isn't something that a phone call could have taken care of. Knowing how fancy and technologically advanced Graham most likely is, I'm surprised he didn't just show up as a hologram. "Is everything okay with Holiday Pies?" Holiday Pies was once just a side business for the family.

Margie Holiday, his grandmother who has since passed on, started with just a single oven and used to bake her famous apple and pumpkin pies to give to her neighbors. Word caught on about how good they were, and soon enough everyone in Gingerbread wanted to buy them. Her success grew so fast that the family opened a factory in Cater, and to this day they mass produce those yummy baked sensations and ship them to a bevy of local grocery stores. His family also owns and operates Holiday Orchards, where they grow fruit and produce. The Holidays are one of Gingerbread's local success stories. They've been referred to as the little-family-that-could for years.

"I have no clue how the pies are doing." He shakes his head, but those day-glow eyes remain pinned on mine. "Tanner doesn't share much with me. Personally, I'm shocked he called a meeting. It's just Mom, Dad, and me. Tanner is something else." He grunts at the thought of his brother. It's a well-known fact Tanner and Graham haven't always gotten along. Graham was closer to Nick than he was his own brother. Tanner, much like his brother, used to be the town playboy, always a different girl next to him at the bar week after week. He's about as interested in Cupid's arrow as he is in his brother. "Anyway"—he scratches at the back of his neck, and his left eye shuts tight—"I need a rental that's furnished. I can't stay with my parents for a month and hang onto my sanity, and I'm pretty sure I'm not staying with Tanner."

"How about Nick?" I volunteer my brother for the effort. "I'm sure he'll let you crash on his couch until your private jet is ready to whisk you back to the Big Apple." I couldn't help but take a swipe at him. Although judging by that blooming grin, it was more of an ego stroke than anything else. And, believe you me, the last thing in the world I want to do is make Graham Holiday gloat over his wild success any more than I have to.

"Nick's out. He's got a bad habit of leaving his dirty socks wherever he pleases, and you know it." He hooks his brow my way, and I can't help but concede with a nod. He is so right about the dirty socks. "Besides, I like the idea of a little solitude. It's a nice break from the big city."

Solitude. I grunt at the thought of such a coveting thing. With both the bakery and my brain on overdrive, I could use a little solitude myself.

I rouse my mother's computer to life and key in the password. "A month off looking for solitude?" I marvel as I peruse the available listings. "My, aren't you a highfalutin fool."

"Come on." His lids lower as those dimples of his dig in, and my insides spike with heat. "Don't tell me you've never wanted to leave Gingerbread."

"I'll have you know, I did leave Gingerbread for two solid years. I went to Arizona, but you wouldn't know that. I doubt you know anything about anyone other than yourself."

"You're right."

I glance back over at him, and he's sporting a goofy grin on his face, same one he used to get just before he pegged me with a zinger.

He leans forward. "Why don't you show me around and tell me about everything I've missed out on? You're still the town gossip, aren't you?"

And there it is. I take a moment to glare at him. "I'm sad to say that Sabrina Jarrett has stolen the title of town gossip right from under me. But I am the town baker now, and I think that's a far better fit for me."

"Baker?"

"That's right. Holly and I opened the Gingerbread Bakery and Café right down the street. We're not raking in a six-figure income like yourself, but we're settled, sort of, and we're really happy about how things have turned out for us."

"*Seven*." He nods as if I should know what this means.

"Seven? Let me guess, that's some cool phrase they say in New York that means something akin to awesome. I've always felt the word *awesome* was a little too West Coast myself." I can't help all the stupid things that are coming from my lips. Graham has always inspired me to spew forth the verbal diarrhea. Usually it's in self-defense, but then, this is Graham. I'm sure things are moving in a defensive direction.

His brows knit together. "Seven figures—as in income. I wasn't trying to pat my back. I was merely correcting you. And I'm happy about the bakery. It sounds like you finally found your calling." He gets that look in his eyes again, and I can feel it coming. "What's better than watching carbs and cash collide? I'll stop by sometime and check it out. I'm always up for a good cookie. You said it was a little shop right down the street?"

My blood hits its boiling point. "I didn't say it was little. It's actually quite *big*—spacious even. Although, I'm pretty sure it's not nearly as big as that space lab you live in. Penthouse, is it?"

He tips his head back as if he were amused. "You seem to know a lot about me, Sprig." Ugh. How I hate that nickname. And even more than that, I detest that he invoked it. I was sort of hoping there was an underlying truce as far as it was concerned. He leans in with that smug look on his face. "Are you keeping tabs?" His left eye comes just shy of winking, and a jolt of rage whips through me. "Let me guess, stalking social media is your favorite pastime."

A breath hitches in my throat, and for a moment I contemplate whether I should throw the granite globe or the bottle of water my mother has sitting on her desk at him.

"I'm not a stalker. And, believe you me, you would be the last person I'd waste my time following. From what I hear, I could get an STD simply by looking you up. No way, no how." I pull up the full report on furnished houses in Gingerbread and gasp.

"What is it?" He drums his fingers over the desk, and it sends my anger skyrocketing. "Let me guess, you're going to need a vaccination. No need to cyberstalk me, sweetie, when I'm seated right in front of you."

"Stop being so incredulous." I try to refresh the listings, but the same stubborn house is the lone wolf to show up to this house-hunting party. "It looks as if there's only one home available."

"Is it furnished, and will they rent month to month?"

"Check and check." And I couldn't be more distraught.

"Well, let's go check it out." He bounces to his feet, and I gather my purse and head to the door. "Don't you want to print it out or jot down the address?"

"No need. I happen to be intimately familiar with the area. I happened to sleep there often." I shoot him a look that stops him in his tracks. "Do not go there." Sometimes you need to put a proverbial muzzle on Graham before he unleashes on you. Although, admittedly, I just about walked into that one. "Let's just say, if you decide to take the place, you'll have the best neighbor."

"Mayor Todd?" He comes in close and wraps an arm around my shoulder as if it belonged there.

"Nope. *Me*." I flash a bitter smile as we walk out the door.

Graham offered to drive us in his rental, and since I arrived on foot from the bakery, I agreed. I was a little surprised to see his fancy rental was a plain old white truck. I was sort of expecting to see a Rolls-Royce Phantom or a Lamborghini Veneno Roadster. There is definitely something homey—and dare I say attractive—about a man who drives a truck, and those are two things I refuse to associate with someone who pretty much amounts to the archnemesis of my childhood.

"We'll be looking at the one on the end." I point over at the Spitzers' place.

Graham grunts with a nod before slowing down and inspecting my own home as if it were suddenly an option. "So, this is your house?" He gives an open-mouthed smile as we drive past my sturdy clapboard home, with its bright red door and oversized green wreath decorating the front of it.

"That's where I call home. I was able to save up enough for a down payment last year. Just moved in back in July, but I pretty much have everything the way I want it." I motion for him to park in the next driveway, and he does. "I've got the lockbox combo, so I can show you the inside. Dave and Marlene have been in Florida for the last few months, and this place has just sat empty. They've become Gingerbread's official snowbirds, leaving at the first sight of a cool breeze. They've pretty much retired and are living out all their white sandy beach fantasies."

Graham takes a deep breath as he inspects the place, and we both get out and take in the fresh Gingerbread air. "So, what are you fantasizing about, Sprig? You still hiding that Barbie collection in a shoebox under your bed?"

My face heats ten shades of crimson as my body prickles with embarrassment. "I'll have you know those dolls are now considered collectors' items, and the only reason they're under my bed is to keep them safe from roving perverts who are thinking about renting the place next door." I take a step into him, and his stark good looks, that midnight black hair, those eyes that look as if they're trying to show the sky up with their color—Graham Holiday's good looks are only magnified with the vast backdrop of snow on the ground. "I bet you're still hiding that Hot Wheels collection in an oversized tire that doubles as a briefcase?" All of the memories of that cute little carryall come flooding back, and I can still smell the sweetness the plastic emitted.

A hearty laugh rumbles from him. I can't help but note the tiny laugh lines around his eyes, and suddenly my insides melt at the sight. Graham isn't the young boy I used to know and detest so much. He's grown into a man in every capacity. And judging by his fast-paced life, he's outgrown Gingerbread by a New York mile. I'm just some backwoods small-town girl to someone like him. Besides, he'll forever see me as Nick Winters' little sister, the girl who braided her Barbie's hair far longer than she ever should have.

"Hot Wheels, huh? *Okay*—I might have a Hot Wheels or two in the attic at my parents' house. Just let me know when your Barbies want to get together with my Hot Wheels. It's a date."

An incredulous laugh huffs from me. "*Please*—I wouldn't date you if you were the last person on earth. I refuse to date people who tugged my hair as if it were a sport. And FYI, I still have a bald spot behind my ear to this day."

His brows bounce in that obnoxious way that lets me know he thinks he's got the upper hand. "What's the matter, Sprig? You still think boys are icky?" He chuckles at his own little dig.

"*Ugh*! Would you please stop calling me that? You do realize I detest that nickname." Sprig is a play on Mistletoe. My formal moniker had been the butt of a few too many jokes when I was in elementary school, so I quickly convinced the entire town to call me Missy. "In fact, I banish you from ever uttering it again. We're grown-ups now, remember? And if you must know, I don't think all boys are icky. Just the one standing in front of me." I lean down and scoop a handful of snow before pelting him with it square in the face. And then I do the only grown-up thing I can think of—run gleefully screaming into the backyard. Dave and Marlene Spitzer's property is parceled off in every direction by a small wooden fence that surrounds the property. It's the last house on the cul-de-sac and butts up to the woods at the edge of town. The thicket behind our homes is the exact reason why I chose this area. I love how quiet and secluded it is. Holly thinks it's spooky up here at night, but I've always appreciated the solitude. I guess that's the one and only thing Graham and I have in common.

"You can run, but you can't hide!" he booms as he comes up from behind, and an icy explosion detonates over my back with a thud. He always did have a killer curveball.

Something small and yellow leaps from the crepe myrtle behind a pile of snow, and my feet stop in their tracks as I let out a blood-curdling scream.

"*Geez*!" Graham runs up panting. "Come on, Sprig. It couldn't have hurt that bad." His eyes are rife with worry as he inspects me for injuries. But before I can spear him with another pointed barb from my tongue, that furry creature does another hop and a leap back behind the crepe myrtle, and this time I all but jump into Graham Holiday's arms as I let out another primal scream. I can tolerate a lot of things, but hairy scary creatures that are practically airborne are not one of them. "Hang on." He picks up a stick and heads to a nearby bush, gently rustling its branches.

A yelp comes from the fence line and then a whimpering cry that sounds anything but hairy scary. In fact, it sounds downright cute.

"Oh my God!" I cry as I struggle to hold myself. "It's gone rabid! It's going to eat us! I'm going to lose a limb to that thing!"

Graham pauses from his pursuit to track it down and frowns over at me. "Are you always this brave, sweetheart?"

"*Always*. And you can drop the sweetheart. Your sweet talking superpowers are faulty with me."

"That's right. I'm icky." He treads in toward the whimpers and heads around the tree, out of my line of vision. "Well, look what we have here." It takes a moment before he emerges, and I gasp at the sight of the cuddly little creature he's holding in his arms. The cutest little blonde puppy in the whole wide world.

"You found a baby!" I squeal as I tiptoe my way over— my go-to move for all things fearful.

"I found a yellow lab is what I found." He gives a gentle scratch behind its ears. "It's a cute girl. They can't stop following me around." He gives a playful wink, and I can't help but groan.

"Give her to me." I'm quick to pull the bundle of joy my way, and I can't help but notice she's shivering. "She's freezing! Who knows how long she's been out here."

"Looks like Dave and Marlene left someone behind."

"No way. They're cat people, and they took Felix with them. I bet you she got in through that hole in the fence." I nod at the opening near the woods. "We'd better get this baby to a vet. I bet there's a family out there who is missing her like crazy."

"I bet you're right."

We head for the driveway, and my mouth falls open. "The house!" After the icy, yet strangely satisfying snowball fight, after discovering the most adorable puppy ever—I almost completely forgot our true intentions. "I could show it real quick if you like?"

"Nope. I'll take it sight unseen. There's a puppy who needs to see a doctor more than I need to see the inside of that place. Besides, I've seen my fair share of bedrooms." That greasy grin of his slides up his face as if he were trying to goad me.

"I'm sure you have. And I'm sure you're gunning to see a lot more."

"You've already turned me down."

"*Please.* Gingerbread is rife with wanton women, and some of them even have egos that match yours." I shed a wide smile because, let's face it, he practically walked into that one. Graham Holiday has an ego the size of the Rocky Mountains. Way back when we were still in school, his ego was so big it needed its own picture in the yearbook.

His brows furrow as if I've sawed on his very last nerve, and then just like that, his affect brightens. "Please tell me you know these wanton women and where can I find them."

Sabrina Jarrett comes to mind with her equally obnoxious ego and self-serving line of banter. My God, it's a match made in pompous heaven.

"You know, come to think of it—I think I do."

Sabrina Jarrett and Graham Holiday deserve one another. I bet sparks would fly just as easily as egos would implode. They'd drive one another bonkers just vying for a spot in the mirror each morning. Sabrina is a spoiled brat who always gets her way, and Graham is an obnoxious playboy who is used to having his ego stroked nightly. She would kill him with her vanity, and he would smother her with his narcissistic ways.

Yes. I think I just found Gingerbread's next *it* couple, and it will be a farce that I will not want to miss. I can't wait to light the fuse and watch the dating dynamite explode right in their faces. Once Sabrina has infiltrated his world, I'm betting Graham won't be able to escape this town fast enough.

We climb back into his truck, and I snuggle in with the sweet little puppy as Graham speeds us off to the vet.

I'm going to sic Sabrina Jarrett on Graham asap.

Joy to the world.

Revenge has come.

It's going to be a holly jolly holiday after all.

Graham

The Gingerbread Vet and Animal Clinic takes us right in as Missy and I wait in a claustrophobic glorified closet for the doctor to arrive.

Missy cradles the playful puppy in her arms as if she were a baby, singing lullabies to her, cooing in her ear, and dotting her fuzzy little forehead with kisses. But it's not the puppy who keeps stealing my attention. It's Missy. I can't get over how grown-up she looks, how striking her features are, and that long milky white hair, those creamy curls, not to mention those dreamy curves. I take a quick breath and step back a moment. Should I be looking at Missy this way? As much as my brain wants to tell me it's wrong, other parts of my anatomy are screaming it's right. Honestly, I've been just about everywhere, seen all types of girls, and Mistletoe Winters is...

"Just beautiful," I whisper.

Missy looks up with those watery lilac eyes. I have never seen another human with those eyes outside of the Winters women.

"She is beautiful, isn't she?" Her features soften as she looks to me with a touch of grief. "I don't think I can part with her if I wanted."

I offer up a quick scratch to the top of the cute pup's head. "I don't think I can either."

The door glides open, ushering in a cool breeze right along with the doctor. "What have we got here?" A slender gentleman with a goatee and glasses breaks out into a grin as soon as he spots Missy with that puppy. "Quite a family you've got." He offers up a wink my way.

Missy gasps a moment. "Oh, actually, we're not a family. We're not even dating. In fact, when it comes right down to it, we can hardly stand one another." She gives a playful wink my way, but I know she's only partially kidding. It's true. Nick and I may have razzed her a little too much over the years, but unlike Holly, Missy always seemed to appreciate the ribbing a bit more. She yelped the loudest, protested far more violently than her sister. In a nutshell, she made it worth the effort, and just the thought brings a twisted smile to my face. It was all in good fun, though, and it sure did sponsor some great memories.

"She's right. We're not dating," I add. "We found the puppy in the back of a home I'm renting."

He tips his head, perplexed a moment. "Dr. Clemson." He shakes both our hands. "I'm new in town, and it's been a pleasure getting to know my neighbors."

"Missy Winters." Her eyes brighten, and my insides heat at the sight of them. I don't remember them being so brilliant in color, so darn stunning to look at. "Welcome to

Gingerbread. I'm sure you'll fit right in." She's quick to greet him. "This is Graham Holiday—who is ironically *on* holiday. He turned in his zip code years ago when he officially gave Gingerbread the boot from his life. He's visiting from New York."

"Nice." He looks my way with an easy smile. "I have a sister in Manhattan."

Missy sputters a tiny laugh, and I know where her dirty mind just went.

"So, the puppy." I'm quick to change the subject in fear Missy's misguided mind might be right. I haven't exactly been holing away in my apartment each night. "How do we go about reuniting it with its rightful owner?"

He takes the tiny bundle of wiggling joy from Missy and performs a quick, routine exam. "She's not chipped, so there's no telling who she belongs to. And we haven't received a single call about a missing puppy. They usually check with the shelter first. I think I'll have my secretary call over. In fact, I'll do just that. Why don't you wait a moment and I'll be right back." He takes off, and Missy scoops the antsy puppy right back into her arms.

"She's shaking!" Missy belts it out as if she just witnessed a beating. "She's completely afraid of that mean old doctor." Her voice reduces to that of a three-year-old.

I can't help but dole out a quiet laugh. "He was plenty nice. And maybe you'd better gird yourself for the fact her owner might come a knockin'." My heart breaks for Missy because I can tell she's already too attached.

The puppy looks up at me with a yelp and practically jumps into my arms.

"Whoa, girl!" I pull up, and she washes my face with her slobbering tongue. "Nothing like wet, sloppy kisses." I pull back with a laugh.

"Bet she's making you feel right at home." Missy doesn't miss a beat with that one.

I choose to ignore her comeback for a moment and look right into this squirmy pup's dark, soulful eyes. "If she doesn't have a home, I'm keeping her."

"You can't keep her." Missy jumps up and warms her body to the tiny beast as if she was a fire. "She's coming home with me."

The door opens again, and Dr. Clemson holds out his hands, exasperated. "Looks as if no one's come forth to claim her."

Missy sucks in a quick breath, and I can practically see the color piquing in her cheeks the way it usually does when she's excited.

Dr. Clemson looks over the file in his hands. "The shelter is full. Unfortunately, we'll have to ship her to Denver. That's her best hope of adoption if her family doesn't come forth."

"You can't send her to Denver." Missy takes the puppy right back and shields her from the both of us. "She'll tremble all the way there. No way, no how. She's coming home with me."

I wince at the thought of this poor thing getting trucked all the way to Denver myself. "How long does her family have to claim her?"

"Well"—the good doctor starts while shaking his head—"there is no real time limit we put on these things, but seeing that she's so healthy and is right where we'd like to see her on the weight scale, I'd say she was well cared for right up until this afternoon."

Missy gives an incredulous huff. "If she was so well cared for, someone would have noticed she was missing by now."

"Or they're at work," I offer, trying to burst her bubble slowly. If the real owner does come by to claim the puppy, he or she is going to have a real fight on their hands.

"I'll keep the puppy." Missy manufactures a stale smile for the doctor.

"Very well. I'd much rather she stay in a loving home, myself. I'll have the secretary draw up the paperwork, and we'll get your information before you go." He takes off, and Missy squeals as if she just won a prize at the carnival.

"Looks like I just got a brand new puppy!"

"No way," I tease as I scoop the exuberant pup back up. "Finders keepers. Besides, she was technically on my property."

"Like you've signed a single paper." She frowns for a moment, but that gorgeous smile blossoms right back.

"Okay, we'll co-parent the dog," I offer. "And when it's time for me to leave, we'll see who she likes best. It's only fair." I can't help but give a greasy grin. I've practically built my childhood around teasing Missy. I don't see why the fun should stop now.

"Fair enough." She shrugs. "You can have her while I'm at the bakery. And once you take off for New York, I'll find someone else to sit with her while I'm away." She coos into those big brown eyes. "Isn't that right, Snowflake?"

"Snowflake?" I pull her back. "No way. She's cool, but she's no Snowflake. How about Sport?"

Missy swats me over the hand. "She's a girl, in the event you weren't paying attention. It's not feminine enough for her. Besides, she's too pretty for that name. She needs something cheery, something that goes with the season. I don't know, something sweet." Her eyes gravitate to a wreath over the back of the door with the word *Noel* written across it in bright red glitter.

"*Noel!*" we shout in unison, each trying to beat the other to the punch.

A laugh gets caught in her throat as she hooks those magical eyes of hers my way. "I guess it's settled then. Noel it is."

"Noel," I repeat as I give the puppy a quick scratch behind the ears. "You have the best name. And you also happen to have the best daddy."

"Ha!" Missy shakes out her curls as she lands a kiss just above the puppy's nose. "Don't you listen to him. You have the best *mommy* is what you have."

"I guess that makes us a family after all," I'm quick to point out.

Her eyes flit to the ceiling. "More like a dysfunctional family."

"Noel Holiday." I rock the playful pup in my arms, and it feels nice. It feels right.

Missy is quick to snatch her from me again. "Noel Winters." She glances my way with that devil-may-care grin blooming on her face. "I think I'll take the rest of the day off and pick up some supplies before we head home." We head out into the reception area, and I start in on the paperwork.

"It looks like Santa came early this year for me," Missy bubbles, and the receptionist chortles right along with her.

"You must have been an awfully good girl," the receptionist chimes.

"You got the awful part right." I couldn't help it. Missy and I have always walked the line of sanity in our relationship. Did I just say relationship?

"Oh, stop." Missy bumps me with her hip. "I've been a very good girl." Those violet eyes hook to mine with an all too familiar look that suggests she's up to something.

Missy might have been a good girl, but something tells me she'll be stepping down from her pedestal long enough to give me heck. And I'm not so sure I mind.

It's starting to feel as if I never left Gingerbread.

As soon as Missy and I do a quick run through Pet Stop and pick up enough food, toys, beds, and blankets for a dozen dogs, I take her home and let her know I'll gladly help pick up her car later. But she assured me it was fine. Holly has a spare key to the bakery van, and she'll bring it by tonight.

Missy mentioned that she'd try to shore up the details on the rental and give me the keys as soon as tonight, so I head over to the Winters Tree Lot to say hello to my oldest friend, her brother.

The scent of evergreens hits hard as I get out of my truck, and I can't help but smile at the bright red sign with block lettering. Nick and I used to run this place together year after year. Of course, Missy and Holly would swing by and help when they could. Missy used to help me collect all the scrap boughs off the ground and weave them into a wreath. My stomach cinches at the memory as if I were grieving it. I'll admit that I've been missing home. The first few years in New York were exactly as exciting as I had hoped they'd be—they were better than I expected them to be. It was wine, women, and wild nights. I lit up the real estate scene as if I were born to run Manhattan. I couldn't have asked for a better reception, but as the years went by, and my visits to Gingerbread dissipated in number, a nagging feeling deep inside of me felt as if something wasn't quite right—as if some vital part of me was missing.

The tree lot is bustling with bodies, families with small children all gravitate to the reindeers corralled in the back, and couples with the looks of sheer enthusiasm cluster around the nobles and firs. I spot a familiar dark-haired dude near the front, closing out a transaction, and I head on over.

"You got any fifty footers? I'm looking to have a bonfire later tonight," I tease, and at least three different people gasp as if I've just threatened to burn down the entire town. Torching a Christmas tree would be tantamount to doing exactly that. "Kidding." I hold up my hands in surrender as Nick belts out a laugh.

"Ignore this clown." He bids his customers a merry Christmas before heading my way and slapping me over the back. "Look what the New York alley cat dragged into town. You swinging by on your way to warmer climates, I hope."

"Nope." I pull him in and pat him on the arm. Any time I'm hanging out with Nick, no matter how much time has elapsed, we pick up right where we left off. "I'm here to stay. One solid month. Tanner called a family meeting, and I'm game to see what it's all about. I'll be at my parents' for dinner. Maybe they'll spill the beans."

"I'll spill them," a familiar husky voice calls from behind, and I startle for a moment as I find my brother staring back at me. Tanner has always been a slightly younger version of myself—by two years to be exact—same strong jaw, dark hair. His eyes don't know the trick to smiling on their own, though. In fact, over the years, Tanner has perfected a scowl that he wears around the clock. It's not a good look if you ask me. "So you're here, huh?" He treks on over, no handshake, no hug, no surprise. "Mom and Dad went to Colorado Springs. They'll be back in a few days."

"Ah." I nod as I give a quick glance to Nick. He's well aware of the strangled tension between Tanner and me. Heck, he's witnessed it firsthand for years. "So the suspense lives on."

"Nope." Tanner takes a breath that expands his chest twice its size, and a part of me wonders if he's trying to intimidate me. "I'm not the type to keep someone hanging." He narrows his eyes my way as if I should know what he's harping about. "I've got the orchard on life support. But soon enough, Holiday Pies will be DOA. As soon as Mom and Dad get back, I'm going to break the news to them, and we're going to close it out with our accountant."

My stomach drops at the thought of losing something that's been in our family for years. "There's no way we're doing that. Let me see the numbers. I'll get a marketing team together, and we'll try to breathe new life into it."

Tanner shakes his head, a dull laugh dying in his chest. "You think you can just ride into town on your white horse, throw a marketing team at the business, and it'll perk right back up? And what happens when you do your yearlong disappearing act once again? Look, Holiday Pies is over. It's dead, and I'm out." He pulls a hundred dollar bill out of his pocket and hands it over to Nick. "That should cover the tree." He takes off for his beat-up old Chevy with the original cherry red paint job faded along with days gone by. It was my grandfather's truck, and Tanner has babied that thing since he was a kid himself.

"You forgot your tree!" I shout over at him, and he turns around. I'm half-expecting him to flip me the bird, but instead, he glowers at me and I can't figure out which is worse.

"Wasn't for me." He hops into his truck and speeds right out of the dirt lot.

Nick stuffs the bill into his front pocket. "It's for the community center. Tanner—Holiday Orchards—donates the tree every year."

I can't help but frown in the direction of my brother's dust. "He might just have a heart yet."

No sooner does any remnant of my brother dissipate than a van with a giant cookie slapped on the side pulls in. The sign reads *Gingerbread Bakery and Café* and, sure enough, a bubbly blonde bounces out, along with an equally perky puppy.

"There's my girl." I head over and scoop Noel up into my arms.

"*Geez.*" Nick comes over and mock socks my arm. "For a second I thought you were talking about my sister. That would have been a friendship killer right there." He gives Noel a quick scratch. "Of course, I'd have to kill you if you were." He flashes a smile at his sister who looks as if she's moved to kill us both.

"Neither of you is funny," she quips before looking to her brother. "But I like your line of thinking."

A bright red Mercedes careens into the lot, and the three of us jump to safety behind a Douglas fir tall enough to fill a two-story building.

A redhead gets out, wrapped in a crimson wool coat and long black boots that hug her legs all the way up to her thighs. Her lips are doused in the same bright color she's sporting, and her eyes widen twice their size once she gets a look at me.

"Well, I'll be—" She waves my way with her creamy white scarf. "Is that you, Graham Holiday?" She does her best to tiptoe over, and her boots have her slipping and sliding all the way here.

Nick catches her by the elbow, and she's quick to bat him away.

"It's been years since my eyes have had a carnal feast with you!" She lunges at me with open arms, and Noel growls and nips at her wrist. "Oh my God!" she howls so loud you'd think she lost an arm in the effort. "Put that beast down!" she cries and backs away as if noticing Noel for the first time. "Like, really, put it down, as in goodnight, sayonara, it's time to take a dirt nap."

"Sabrina Jarrett!" Missy is quick to cover Noel's floppy ears with her hands. Then just as quickly as her temper flared, she takes Noel from me and forces a smile. "Now, maybe you don't care for dogs of the canine kind, but I'm betting you have more than a hankering for the human variety and, believe you me, there is no dirtier dog than Graham Holiday." She takes a moment to sneer my way. "Nick?" She does her best to blink innocently at her brother, but I know Missy far too well to realize there isn't one innocent thing about her intentions. "You mind helping me see how Noel does with the reindeer?"

"You bet."

Missy puts Noel down and holds onto the leash for the ride as Sabrina and I watch them speed toward the fun zone.

"No use in watching from afar." I tick my head toward the corral filled with Santa's motorcade. "I'm betting Noel steals the show from every creature Nick has tucked in this place. Can't wait to see the smile on those kids' faces."

A wretched groan comes from her as she hooks her arm through mine. "Dogs and kids are right up there with insects and vermin. Why don't you help me pick out a tree for my living room? I'm thinking a noble about twelve to fifteen feet." She leans in close, her long lashes doing their best to bat their way into my good graces. "Like I say, go big"—she runs her hand up over my biceps—"and you are big—and then take them home." She licks her lips with a promise, and it hits me. It was no coincidence that Missy showed up a second before Sabrina here ambled out of her fancy ride. I glance back to the corral and, sure enough, Missy's eyes are feasted on the two of us. Nick is in the pen with Noel, and Missy couldn't care less. She's here for a show, and something tells me it's this one. If Missy wants a show, I'll make sure she gets one.

I wrap an arm around Sabrina and give Missy a little wave, and her mouth falls open. She gives an awkward flick of the fingers my way, and I can't help but feel a smug sense of satisfaction. Something isn't right, and I'm about to get to the bottom of it.

One thing is for sure.

Mistletoe Winters is most definitely up to no good.

2

Naughty is the New Nice

Missy

A light sprinkling of snow dusted the ground this morning, just enough to refresh that shaken snow globe appeal Gingerbread holds so strong to. Mother Nature would hate to displease the tourists with a town filled with slush and a muddy river running down Main Street. I'd have to agree with her there.

It's day three of sharing Noel with Graham—my official new neighbor. I've been taking the brunt of the sleepless nights, and he has the carefree mornings and afternoons when she's reduced to a playful, cuddly pile of fluff.

I frown over at my sister, Holly, without meaning to. We've just wrapped up a two-hour session of working on those gingerbread monstrosities, and right about now, we're both seeing gingerbread stars. The bakery is bustling, the ovens are on nonstop, and it's a hot house in here.

Holly wrinkles her nose at the dueling dollhouses. "Whose idea was it to build a Barbie mansion out of flour and molasses?"

"Yours," I flatline. It's true. Holly came up with the idea after her daughter, Savanah, said she'd love to climb inside one of our standard gingerbread houses—the ones that you could no more stick your foot in let alone a body. "But you were right. It's going to be a big hit, and I know Mayor Todd's twins are going to love, love, *love* it." I try to muster up the enthusiasm she exuded when she spoke those exact words to me a month ago.

"Are you kidding?" She leans into the chrome alongside the freezer and does a quick check of her mulberry stained lips. "Savanah is trying to convince Todd to purchase the one up for auction. And if the price on that thing skyrockets the way I'm thinking it will, we'll be homeless if we win it."

"You tell Savy to put it on her Christmas list. I bet she's got a crazy aunt who would pull a few late nights to make sure all of her gingerbread dream house wishes come true."

"What about Noel?" Her brows arch into her forehead as her concern for my sweet pooch rises. Holly is just as in love with Noel as I am.

"She has a daddy. And, believe me, it wouldn't hurt said daddy to experience the pain of a few sleepless puppy nights once in a while. That alone will abolish all thoughts of stealing Noel away to Manhattan once he's through with Colorado. Besides, Noel would hate living in a penthouse—what with all the dog walkers, being forced to jog through Central Park rain or shine? I bet they don't even give their dogs water out there. They go straight for the caffeinated stuff. Starbucks on tap."

Holly sighs with a dreamy look on her face. "Do you think I can get Graham to take me back to New York with him? I bet I can convince that dog walker to make a left on Fifth Avenue. And, if I asked real nicely, I bet Graham would give me all access to his American Express Black Card."

A breath gets caught in my throat at the thought of Graham having something so exclusive, so breathtakingly dangerous as a credit card with no legal limit. "Wow"—I marvel with a dark laugh—"did I *ever* set Sabrina Jarrett up with just the right guy."

"What!" Holly squawks so loud half the customers crane their necks this way. Jenna gives a subtle wave for us to keep it down. Thank heavens for Jenna and the extra hands on deck. Holly and I would never be able to manage this place on our own. But more helping hands means more paychecks to write, and with frenemies like Sabrina eating away all our profits, who needs to stay open?

"Don't *what* me." I glance out toward the indoor patio where Sabrina is hosting yet another book club meeting, the one in which they discuss their next juicy romp through literature. I know more about the workings of Sabrina's social clubs than I do the workings of the lumberyard—and the lumberyard has been in my family for years. "Look at her." I nudge my sister in the shoulder as we stare over at the redheaded hellion laughing it up while stuffing her face with a handful of hazelnut crinkle cookies that I just pulled out of the oven this morning. As soon as she saw me loading those delectable delights onto the tray, she demanded three batches—my *entire* inventory. "Do you think she cares about the price of hazelnuts this time of year? No. Sabrina is a drain on our budget, and the sooner we find someone to take her off our hands the better off we'll be financially. You might even be able to buy a real dollhouse for Savanah. Who knows? She and Graham might even fall in love. If he happens to whisk her off to New York for good, you won't find me shedding a tear."

"Ditto to that." Holly digs her fists into her hips as she tilts her head toward Sabrina and the book tour she's sponsoring. "I don't know. I guess I always thought you and Graham might end up together one day."

"*What?*" My entire body bucks in protest. "And live a life full of torment and misery while you grow happily old with Todd? I'd pull my hair out before I was thirty. And I'd lose my sanity long before that. Nope. Graham Holiday and I are *not* destined to be together. Trust me, I know these things. I have a gift, remember? You'd think I'd be the first to realize it if he were the one for me." My stomach clenches as if I just spewed a bucket full of lies, and I can't help but glare at it a moment. My phone goes off, and it's a text from Graham himself.

Headed to Angelino's for a quick bite. Want to join me? Nick's babysitting Noel. Is that okay with you, Mom?

"Ha!" I balk at his text as I share it with Holly. "He's already clocking out on the job. Clearly, he's not cut out to be a father. And lucky for him, Sabrina wants nothing to do with anything in its infantile stages—puppy or human."

I start to text back, then stop cold. "Wait a minute. I shouldn't be the one meeting up with him at Angelino's. I think there's a certain redheaded super-charged diva who is more than willing to fill my stilettos while scarfing down pizza with Graham."

"You don't wear stilettos," Holly is quick to point out, and I scoff at her as I type up a reply.

"Head on over. I'll try my best to make it!" I read my response out loud as I hit *Send*, and he replies in less than a second.

Already here.

"Well then." I look to my sister. "Let the fun begin!"

"Oh, what are you up to?" A string of worry lines appears on her forehead, and I flick them with my finger as I stride on past her. "Ow! I hate it when you do that."

"You'll thank me when you're line-free at sixty." I head to the counter and wave Sabrina over from her cackling session. I spot the treats piled high on their table and note the hazelnut crinkle cookies have already been devoured. In their place sits a small mountain of snowcapped brownies. It takes everything in me not to overturn the tray of sugar cookies in front of me. The snowcapped brownies are made with only the best ingredients, one of them being chocolate chips imported from Belgium.

Sabrina huffs and puffs her way over, her discontent with me only growing in exaggeration with every stomping step. Sabrina is the epitome of a three-year-old in a grown woman's body. I honestly can't see the appeal she holds to that motley crew of hers.

"What is it?" she snips. "Do you have a book recommendation? Because if you don't have a book rec, I don't see the point of this little tête-à-tête. There are book boyfriends to be had, and we're in the process of hunting them down."

"I don't have a book rec *or* a book boyfriend—but I have something far better. A *real* boyfriend waiting for you at Angelino's across the street. He's only the world's handsomest, wealthiest, biggest success story that Gingerbread has ever seen."

She sucks all of the oxygen out of the room with one enormous breath. "You mean Graham Holiday is waiting for me?"

I give an eager nod. "And as the official and most *proficient* matchmaker just this side of the Rockies, let me tell you that he is undoubtedly the one for you." I may not be all that proficient, but Sabrina doesn't need to know that. All she needs to know is that Graham Holiday officially has a target on his back, and I've just turned her into a torpedo. "I promise that you and Graham will be the premier super couple in all of Gingerbread. Once I gift you Graham Holiday's head on a platter, there will be no refuting it."

Her mouth falls open as she looks to herself in the mirror to our left. "This is really happening." She primps her hair with her fingers. "I can't believe this, Missy. I have wanted Graham Holiday for myself for as long as I can remember."

"Well, here's your chance. Would you like a few insider tips on how to land your man?"

She inches back. The look on her face lets me know that projectile vomiting half the bakery she just inhaled is a real possibility. "From *you*?" She breaks out into a pitiful laugh. "Oh, *honey*. I'm thankful you pointed my feet in the right direction, but let's face it—I can take it from here. No offense, but taking advice from you would be like the choir instructor asking the church mouse for a few instructions. Back up and watch a seasoned pro. I'll have a rock on this finger by New Year's." She wiggles her left hand my way as she heads back to her page turning posse.

My stomach does an odd revolution, and as much as I try to tell myself the visual of Sabrina upchucking my cookies was the leading cause, the thought of Graham decorating her finger with bling makes my insides churn.

I look to Holly who's busy scowling at me.

"Oh, who cares?" I hiss. "It's a means to an end. They deserve each other, remember?"

"Okay." She tosses her hands in the air before unleashing herself from her apron. "Just remember you deserve someone, too."

Sabrina races out the door and into traffic. The sound of a car horn cuts through the silence.

Holly shakes her head. "Wind her up and watch her go."

"Are you kidding?" I scramble to take off my own apron. "You and I are about to get front row seats."

I shout for Jenna to man the fort as I pull Holly by the wrist all the way there.

Angelino's is a quaint Italian restaurant with a pizza bar that lines the front as well as tables and booths in the back. It's one of Gingerbread's official fast casual restaurants that you can get in and out of pretty quickly if you just want to sneak a bite between batches of cookies baking in the oven. They have a popular sandwich counter that usually has a line out the door at lunchtime, and they're our only hope for delivery in the evenings.

Holly and I step inside and are immediately welcomed by the thick scent of garlic and roasted marinara as they permeate the air. I take a deep breath in through my nose and savor the scents as my stomach begins to growl.

"There he is!" Holly gasps as she points to the back where a bewildered Graham Holiday tries to decode whatever Sabrina is pumping in his ear.

"Ha! The look on his face is priceless!" I pull my sister into a booth near the front, affording us a full view of the soon-to-be lovelorn couple in the rear of the establishment.

A waiter comes over with a basket of complimentary garlic breadsticks, and Holly quickly orders a large veggie pizza.

I snap my fingers to get his attention before he leaves. "Throw on a slice of Canadian bacon and pineapple for me!"

Holly waves me off. "You don't throw on a slice once you order a whole pizza. Weirdo." She ducks for a moment as Sabrina's piercing laughter resonates through the place.

"Sure you can." My voice wavers as I say it. "That way you and Tom can have a pizza for dinner, and I won't feel bad about cutting into it." I glare over at the table in the back as the two of them laugh it up as if they were having the time of their lives. How dare they have so much fun, and right in front of my face! The whole idea was to invoke a serious dose of misery on both parties—or at least Graham.

"Why are you shooting them dirty looks?" Holly pulls my hand over until I'm forced to look at her.

"Because the point of this wasn't to have them enjoying one another's company. I wanted Sabrina to slowly kill Graham with her homicidal laughter, not have him join in on it."

Her mouth rounds out as she gives an awkward nod in their direction. "He's coming this way!"

Graham's woodsy cologne arrives at the table long before he does, and I can't help but inhale the warm scent and let it fill my lungs for a moment. I've always been a sucker for a clean-smelling man, just not this particular one.

"Holly." He nods to my sister. "Missy, can I speak with you alone for a minute?"

"*No*," I shoot back so fast it sounds like a reprimand. "I mean, we've only got a few minutes left on our lunch break, and we're just starving to death."

I jam half a breadstick into my mouth and moan as if it were a decadent slice of cheesecake. But it's not. It's dry toast smeared with garlic salt, and it's all I can do not to gag right in his face. It would serve him right after he all but enjoyed Sabrina's company in my presence. As if him standing right in front of me isn't vexing enough, he's practically gloating over the fact he's having a great time. No way am I going to let him haul me to the side to let me in on it either. I've got two eyes. I can see what's going on here.

Graham folds those enormous arms of his across his wide as a linebacker's chest. "Have it your way." He tucks his pointy tail back between his legs and heads back to the redheaded demon waiting to greet him. I can't help but scowl at the two of them as they pick up right where they left off—in Happyville.

Holly makes a face. "Have what your way? You think he's onto you?"

"Who cares?" I pick the remainder of my breadstick apart as if I were readying a crumb trail to lead to the bakery. "What matters most is that the two beating hearts seated in that direction find their way to beating as one. I'll be right there at their wedding, ready and willing to tackle anyone who objects."

"*Aw!*" Holly mocks me while looking destitute at the thought. The pizza arrive, and neither of us bothers digging in. "I can't believe you're really letting a prize like Graham Holiday go to waste to someone who doesn't even eat *pie*." She leans in. "She doesn't eat PIE! What kind of a person is that?"

I wrinkle my nose over at Sabrina a moment. "She's subhuman. We both know that. But Graham doesn't seem to mind." I openly glare over at him as he nods into her ridiculousness. "I'm betting that whole pie thing isn't a deal breaker to someone like him." Graham is so rich he could hire someone to eat pie as he watches. In fact, I bet he compiles an entire list of the ridiculous ways he wastes his money.

"It should be a deal breaker." Holly pulls a slice off the platter, and the mozzarella strings itself right to her mouth. "Mmm," she moans. "So good. *Hey*! If Graham and Sabrina get married, they should totally have Angelino's cater their wedding. It's where they had their first official date, after all. And, of course, we'll provide the cake—for free." She rolls her eyes because, face it, it's pretty much a given.

"I didn't think about that one." I spin my plate and watch my pizza turn upside down. "At that point, it will be a good riddance cake as well." I steal another glance their way, and my appetite is no longer anywhere to be found. For whatever reason, Graham Holiday is invoking all sorts of emotions in me ever since he's dropped back into Gingerbread, and I'm not too sure I like it.

In fact, I know I don't.

Sabrina continues to cackle at Graham long after Holly and I box up our food.

I guess I am a pretty decent matchmaker.

After all, I'm still batting a thousand.

Too bad it doesn't feel half as good as I thought it would.

Saturday night, long after the bakery is closed—long after I've tuckered myself out trying to spy on my newfound next-door neighbor, I decide to get dressed and head back out into the cold, dark world. All of his lights are out, and he hasn't been home since I picked up Noel. He didn't mention he was going out. Although he did look a little haggard, handsomely so. It's not fair that even in his slightly disheveled, frustrated-with-the-world state, he still looks as if he should be selling underwear in print ads high above Manhattan. Anyway, he went out. And the fact he's out and I'm home makes me feel ten times more like the old maid Holly keeps telling me I am. So I do the only thing I can. I put Noel on a leash, bundle up, and head for the tree lot. Really, I have no business staying home nights, not nights in December anyway. Nick needs all the assistance he can get this time of year. And with Holly home helping Savanah with her homework, Dad breaking his back at the lumberyard all day—thus basically incapacitated by four o'clock, and a mother who wouldn't be caught dead at the tree lot in general, I'm his only hope as far as the family goes. It's just Nick and a couple of high school kids he's hired working it on their own.

The air is frosty as a snowman, yet the wind thankfully died down. I've donned my warmest scarf and a ski jacket. And I've even put on a pair of doggie booties for Noel to wear so the snow doesn't freeze her paws right off. The poor thing slips and slides her way out of the car as we head into the lot. I've got her bundled up as well in a nifty little Christmas sweater I bought at the Bow-Wow-Tique next to Pet Stop. It's red and garish with a picture of a cat smoking a cigar while poking its head through a wreath. It's the epitome of an ugly sweater, and I love every last hideous stitch about it.

"Whoa, whoa, whoa," a deep voice calls from the front, and my mouth falls open as I find Graham headed this way with a Santa hat planted over his head.

So this is where he went! Of *course*, he did. He's always helped Nick this time of year, or he used to anyway. I guess there's still some Gingerbread spirit left in Graham after all. Go figure.

He pauses shy of me and moans at the sight of Noel. "What did you do to my poor dog?" He scoops her up and begins plucking off her boots.

"That might be your dog, but that's also my baby girl." I run around snapping all the cute pink booties off the ground. "Hey, these things cost money. Some of us don't have a tree in our living room that sprouts Benjamins, you know."

"I'll have you know I have to work for them myself." He plucks at Noel's snug red sweater before abandoning the effort and shaking his head my way while placing her back on the ground. She starts sniffing around, jumping and chomping at the bit to run right to the reindeer. "Looks like someone misses her friends. Nick says they get along great. Let's take her on a playdate, shall we?" He hands me the leash.

I glance behind him and spot Nick helping out a client. "Fine," I say as if he forced me into the idea, and the two of us make our way through a labyrinth of trees. Nick has a large tent set up that has always reminded me of a circus that houses a small sampling of trees in the event inclement weather prevents people from stalking out into the wild to pick their perfect evergreen. As a little girl, I'd dance a jig on the day that beautiful red and white tent went up, and my heart always broke a little on the day it came back down. The trees outside of the tent are legion, and, of course, are fair game to customers as well. With literally acres of nobles and firs to choose from, the Winters Tree Lot has inspired people to drive from all over this region of Colorado.

"So, what brings you to the lot?" he asks as we slow our pace. "You could have easily been snuggled up by a fire reading this little girl a bedtime story, and yet you chose to dress her funny and parade her around in this, a public display of misguided affection. It's really quite humiliating for her. I hope you're committed to paying for doggie therapy once she hits her teens."

A light laugh bounces from me. "So you do admit she's mine." I can't help but boast a gloating smile. "I called Dr. Clemson this morning, and he said no one has stepped forward to claim her yet. I told him that if they did, they'd have a legal battle on their hands for neglect. There's no way I would let those louses have this sweet baby girl back. Do they have social workers for dogs? Because if they don't, that should totally be a thing."

Graham belts out a laugh just as we hit the corral in the back, and instantly Noel is flooded with a sea of toddlers who have all but abandoned their efforts at peeking at Santa's snow patrol.

"She's loving this!" I give a little hop as Noel licks up every little hand and face in turn. Several of their parents begin snapping pictures of her, so I let the leash go, and we watch as Noel does her thing. "Would you look at that? She's a natural!" I glance over to Graham and do a double take. He's not paying one bit of attention to Noel. He's too busy looking at me. "What?" I touch my fingers to my cheek. "Do I have frosting on my face? In my defense, I was icing what amounts to the Empire State Building, and I'd better not say that too loud or Mayor Todd will have me building a replica of it for next year's auction."

"No," he says it soft as his eyes gently caress my features. "You look perfect." He tips his head toward the tiny cookie and cocoa stand set up to our right. It's something

Holly and I came up with when we were in high school. We would man it and make all the cookies and cocoa ourselves. I guess you could say this is the predecessor to the bakery. We've been baking our way to our destinies for quite some time now. There's a bright red sign next to it that reads *Get Your Reindeer Feed Here!* "How about I buy you a cup of something hot?" he offers. "And if you're good, I might throw in a cookie."

We head over a few feet, and I don't dare take my eyes off Noel. But for the most part, she's doing her impression of the world's most perfect yellow lab—actually freezing like a statue for pictures and keeping her head pointed at the camera.

"Geez," I marvel. "She's better at taking pictures than Savanah is. Don't tell my sister I said that." Although Holly would be the first to agree with me. I've been to almost all of Savy's yearly photo shoots since she was one, and not once has she decided to cooperate with the photographer.

Graham strums a husky laugh as he exchanges his dollars for hot cocoa and hands me a mug with three pink marshmallows floating on top.

He takes a quick sip from his and moans. "That's delicious."

"It should be. I made it." I point over to the candy cane cookies and ask for four. "Here." I hand two over to Graham as we amble over to the fence while watching Noel. "You're more naughty than you are nice, but I'm giving you a couple of treats anyway."

He makes a face. "I'm nice. You just don't realize it."

"*Ha*! I don't realize it because it's never been displayed. Name one nice thing you've done all night."

"I just paid for your cocoa. And I upped the value of your home by moving in next door. Nobody likes a deadbeat area filled with abandoned houses. You're welcome." He toasts me with his cocoa before taking a bite out of his cookie. "Wow, you are good. I'll have to come by and sample my way around that shop of yours."

"Why not?" I toss my hand in the air, exasperated. "Everybody else is doing it."

"Like who?" His brows pin together in the middle and do their best impression of a bird in flight. Graham has always had the most mesmerizing dark full brows. Nothing busy beyond repair that you wish someone might landscape, perfect dark lines that expressed his every thought. I'll admit that I have always been spellbound by those caustic blue eyes of his. It's easy to get lost in them. Sort of like I'm doing now.

"Like that new girlfriend of yours." I can't help but bite down on a devious smile. I'm going to hear it here first. Graham Holiday has a girlfriend, an official plus one who he will gleefully haul out of town for me come December twenty-sixth. Best Christmas present ever. Not a single soul in Gingerbread will be lamenting over the void Sabrina will leave behind. Graham and Sabrina will get their unhappily ever after, and I'll be the one with a happy ending.

My stomach sours as if maybe I won't.

Graham takes a deep breath, and his chest expands the width of a door. He rocks back on his heels a moment as he stares out into space. "I don't have a girlfriend."

"Sure you do. I saw the two of you whooping it up at Angelino's the other day, remember? You opened your mouth, and she laughed at whatever came out. If that's not a sign of true love, I don't know what is." My body bucks with a silent laugh. How I wish I could replay that look on his face when he stomped his way to my table. Honestly, that look of horror was worth the entire effort.

He grunts as he chomps down on his cookie again, this time with a marked aggression. "Sabrina is a handful, but that's all she is to me." He looks me over with a wry smile. "At the moment."

My stomach sinks like a stone, and I force myself to clear my throat. "So, what about back home? I bet you have twelve maids a-milking, all waiting for you in that expansive living room of yours." I can picture it now. A bevy of scantily clad beauties all primping away for the moment their prince strides back to town on his white 747 steed.

"You really think you're funny, don't you?" He blinks a smile my way. "I don't have anyone I'm serious about back there either." He looks to Noel as she does her best to squirm under the fence.

"*No!*" I shout, and Graham gently lands his hand over mine as I try to reach for her. A lot of good that would have done. I'm standing a good fifteen feet away. "I swear, half the time she thinks her name is No."

"She's fine." He lands a warm hand over my back, and I can feel him vibrate with a dull laugh right down to my toes. "I let her run around in there during the day. It helps get all that extra energy out. That way she's nice and tuckered out for you when you get home." His dimples dig into his cheeks, and my stomach bites with heat. Darn Graham for bringing all his big city charm and his alarmingly handsome face back to Gingerbread.

"You do that for me?" I give him a playful shove in the chest and note it's hard as the Rock of Gibraltar. My God, is he bench-pressing all of Wall Street in his spare time?

"Yes, I do that for you." His head inches back a notch as if stunned I'd even ask.

I clear my throat. "So you never answered the question. How many girls are you juggling back home? And do the ladies of the night prefer to be called *women* instead of *girls*?"

His brows knit as he warms his shoulder to mine, his hand still at home over the small of my back. "You're really not funny, and to answer your question, none. There were a few who tried to rope me, but I got away."

For a second I picture Graham running around exclusive nightclubs trying to escape an entire herd of girls with spinning lassos in hand.

"Have you gone out with any of these people more than once? Like say, *three* times? I'm pretty sure in a big city like New York that qualifies as an engagement."

He laughs into the night, and something warms in me just to hear it. I used to do anything short of juggling monkeys on fire just to hear that sound once upon a time.

"I guess so. A girl at the office." He grimaces at the thought of her. "She's actually put in the greatest effort to tie me down, but I've put up quite the resistance."

"*Ooh*, I like her already." I don't, but that's beside the point. "She doesn't fool around. What's her name?"

"Cynthia Caldwell"—he holds a finger in the air—"of the Upper East Side Caldwells."

We share a laugh on behalf of Cynthia's entire family.

"She sounds very Upper East Side and sophisticated." I give a little shrug and tuck my cocoa close to my lips. No matter how hard I tried, I'm sure I couldn't fit into New York high society. Graham could easily. He's always had a mass appeal and been a little more refined than the rest of us.

"Sophisticated?" His brows peak. "That she is. She's also very insistent on getting her way. And you might say she's a part of the reason I had to make a side trip to Colorado this winter. A person can only duck and evade so much."

A boisterous laugh bubbles from me. If only he knew the ducking and evading he is in for with Sabrina. I'm pretty sure she'll make Cynthia Caldwell from the Upper East Side wish she could hide between the racks at Bloomingdale's. Sabrina is a master at getting what she wants, and right now she wants nothing more than this handsome buck by my side.

"What's this?" My brother strides over with that overgrown PVC pipe we use to measure the length of the trees, and it towers next to him like an unstable staff.

"Hey, Nick." I struggle to get his name out as my laughter dies down. "Just having some fun." I wipe a tear from my eye. A part of me wants to fast-forward this entire Sabrina Jarrett fiasco just to see Graham trying to duck and evade with the best of them. Of course, by then, it'll be too late, and Sabrina will be snug in his penthouse. Believe you me, she'll be more difficult to get rid of than an entire herd of New York sewer rats.

Nick narrows his eyes over the two of us as a family to his left gets antsy for his attention.

"Don't have too much fun." He pegs the two of us with a silent warning, and I can't help but avert my eyes. My brother has spent his twenty-nine years on this planet making sure my chastity stays right where it belongs, and some might say—*Holly*—that he's doing too good of a job. Nick has pretty much scared off every single prospect I've ever had as far as men are concerned. I'm sure he'd be more than content if I were an old spinster with a house full of obese cats.

"Don't you worry, Nick. We're not having any fun at all. In fact, let the record show that Graham Holiday is the last person on the planet I could possibly have any fun with."

"We'll see." He looks to Graham. "You'd better steer clear of her if you do want to have any fun. She's not only a premier baker, but she's the best matchmaker this side of the Mississippi, and it just so happens to be her busy season with both." Nick takes off with his jaw set in a scowl, clearly unconvinced by my declaration, but judging by that sour expression on Graham's face, he's more than a believer.

"It's not possible for us to have any fun," I repeat firmly as a fact. "Isn't that right?" I bat my lashes up at him, and he takes a breath.

"Anything you say, Sprig." His cobalt eyes catch over mine, and a fire rakes through me.

"You know I hate that nickname."

"Yeah"—he slings his arm around my shoulders as we watch Noel jump and leap as she chases the reindeer to and fro—"but you know you love me."

"All ego all the time. What's not to love?" I take a bite from my cookie and swallow down a laugh because suddenly the moment grows all too serious. I shake myself out of the trance that his eyes keep trying to suck me into and force myself to stare into the corral.

Soon enough, Graham will realize what a catch he has in Sabrina, and he'll whisk her away to the other side of the country. That should be the only thing I focus on. For sure I shouldn't be focusing in on Graham Holiday's ocean blue eyes.

Nope. Graham belongs to Sabrina. He is simply a means to a blissful Sabrina-free end.

Isn't he?

Graham

On a snowy Monday afternoon, my parents finally make the trek back to Gingerbread, and it's a somewhat joyous reunion as we meet up in front of the Gingerbread Bakery and Café. I say it's somewhat joyous because Tanner just arrived with that permanent scowl he has etched on his face. He wanted to meet at the diner down the street, but I volunteered Missy's new place, which isn't really new after all. I can't believe how much I've missed in her life. Not that I was ever a central figure, but, to be honest, it sure felt like it. Missy and I shared some good times even if she is the last person who would ever admit it.

"Look at you!" My mother squeezes my cheeks tight as if I were three. It's always been her favorite go-to move whenever I make a reprisal. She buries her dark hair in my neck a moment as she comes in for an awkward power hug. It's my mother who gifted Tanner and me our dark hair and blue eye combo. My father used to have the same dark hair— a little more red thrown in the mix—but he's more or less a silver fox now. His eyes are darker than soot, and my mother likes to say it was his button eyes that she fell in love with. And he just so happens to be the kindest soul on the planet, not a single grain of soot in a single one of his cells if you ask me.

Mom grunts as she looks up at me. "You are just more handsome than ever. How has anyone not snagged you off the market yet?" She glances to my brother with her lips twisted in a knot. "I'm telling you, one of these days, one of you is going to have to give me a daughter-in-law."

"Don't look at me," Tanner grumps as he makes his way into the bakery, and as soon as he opens the door, the sweet scent of vanilla wafts out to greet us.

Dad nods my way as he holds open the door. "Let's get in before we catch our deaths out here."

"Oh, that's not possible." Mom waves him off before glancing my way with a scolding look. "Gingerbread winters are good for the soul, young man. Don't you forget it."

We head in, and I soak in the sights. The Gingerbread Bakery and Café is painted a pale green with pink bakery boxes dotting the counters as well as stacked in the back as far as the eye can see. Garland shimmering in gold and red is strung from the ceiling and skips across the expansive room. An entire indoor patio sits to our right with curved windows like the ones my parents have in their sunroom. The café is laden with customers, and there are at least a half dozen children with their noses pressed to the glass cases that hold all the sugary treats. I marvel at the selection for a moment. How hard Missy and Holly must have to work to make all of this magic happen. For a moment, I'm in awe of their dedication.

Mom finds us a seat smack in front of the counter, and I can't help but crane my neck, looking for signs of my favorite baker, Mistletoe Winters. She's been giving me a hard time, and I've lapped up every minute of it.

"Who are you looking for?" Dad joins me in craning my neck.

"No one." I glance to Tanner because a part of me senses he knows better. "I was just admiring those towering gingerbread houses in the back." I nod to the pair of twin overgrown breaded homes that must have taken weeks to assemble. In all of my life I've only put together one of those monstrosities, and it was on a much smaller scale. I was in grade school and forced to do it. I vowed never to venture into the culinary arts ever again. And true to my word, I haven't. I think it's best for everyone that way.

"Right, gingerbread houses." Tanner knocks over the table as if calling the meeting to order, and just as he does it, both Holly and Missy appear from the back. The sisters exchange a brief glance as they spot me, and I offer a polite wave in reciprocation.

Missy grabs a tray of something from the refrigerated section and heads on over. "The entire Holiday clan!" she sings. "To what do I owe the pleasure?" She lands the tray of cookies on the table, and my mouth waters to take a bite from them all. "Please enjoy these white chocolate holiday cookies on the house. A round of coffee for anyone?"

"Yes, please!" Dad raises a finger.

"You're a lifesaver!" Mom chimes. "And thank you for the treats. You know you didn't have to do that. But since you did, please stop by the Knit Wit for a free knitting lesson anytime! I keep telling your mother we need to teach you young girls the art of knitting so you can carry on the tradition. It's never too late to learn."

Missy nods, and I can't help but note how her skin glows in the light. Back in New York, Cynthia glowed, too, like an alien. She said it was a strobing effect she was actually shooting for. But Missy isn't glowing like an alien. She's more of an angel—with horns well hidden, but an angel nevertheless. Her red sweater offsets those lavender eyes, and I can't help but openly stare at how beautiful she is. Growing up, Missy was always pretty, but fast-forward a few pages into the calendar, and Mistletoe Winters is an outright stunner. She's a bona fide knockout, and if she were in New York for a minute, she'd have every eligible stockbroker panting after her. I've seen them panting over all of the pretty young things that make their way to the city and claiming the crème of the crop. Missy definitely qualifies as the crème, but there's no way I'd let one of those wolves roaming Wall Street take a bite out of her.

"And coffee for you?" She looks to Tanner and me, her eyes lingering a moment too long my way.

"Coffee," Tanner grunts like he's in need of an IV full of the caffeinated beverage, and knowing my brother, he is. I know he's working sun up until sun down, but he volunteered for the effort, so I don't feel too sorry for him.

"Same." I nod. "And don't worry about Noel. Nick's fine with her at the lot. He says she sells twice as many trees as anyone with two legs." It's true. As soon as we got there, he strapped a bright red bow on her collar and put her straight to work.

"That's our baby girl!" Missy belts out a laugh as she takes off.

Mom tugs at my elbow. Her mouth droops as if she were about to be let in on a juicy tidbit of gossip. "What's this?"

Tanner leans in. "They're sharing a dog. Now, are we ready to talk business, or should we ogle over the golden child a few minutes longer?" He raises a tired brow, and I'm bewildered by the dig. Tanner has referenced me as the *golden child* before, but that's when we were kids and never in public. It's as if he's belligerent with his disdain for me, and for the life of me I can't figure out why. We hardly speak. I couldn't stay further away from him if I tried. I'm amused at how exactly it is that I'm annoying him from afar.

"What's your problem, dude?" I shoot him a look. "Haven't I stayed out of your hair long enough? You can't handle me for five simple minutes?"

He closes his eyes a moment as Dad whispers a quiet reprimand for us to keep it down.

"*Dude*"—Tanner mocks me with his tone—"your ability to stay out of my hair seems to be the problem." He flashes a lightning quick smile before turning to my parents. "Look, I let Graham in on this last week. Holiday Pies is over. It's been a good run—fifteen years. Grandma lived to see her dream take flight, but now she's gone, and unfortunately, so is the business. I think it's time we shut down the factory and call it a day."

A hard gasp comes from behind, and I turn to find Missy with her mouth opened wide, a carafe full of coffee precariously ready to spill.

"I heard nothing!" She sets down a tray of coffee and disperses it before taking off for the counter again.

She heard enough, and to be honest, I have, too.

Mom lets out a wild groan. "Why on earth can't we keep it? Isn't it bringing everyone joy? I have never met a soul who said they didn't enjoy your grandmother's pies. And the local grocery stores seem happy to stock them."

Tanner winces. "They are, Mom. And they're also happy to order less and less every month. It's just not selling well. The public voted with their dollars, and they're not interested."

"It can't be true," Dad protests. "What's Christmas in Gingerbread without a Holiday pie?"

Tanner looks to me as if searching for help. "Business is great in Gingerbread, but even here we're only selling a couple dozen pies. Places like this have come in with far more exciting desserts to offer, and they're fresh baked at that."

Another gasp comes from behind the counter, and I spot Missy ducking once I glance her way. I can't help but shed a tiny smile, although at the moment there's not much to smile about. My brother is right. Everyone is doing it better, and now we're about to pay the price.

Dad takes an even breath. "So, what do you propose we do about this? There has to be some way we can save Holiday Pies."

Tanner looks to me as if I might have the answer. "Perhaps there was a way, but since the entire operation was saddled on me alone, it sank. The truth is, I can't run the orchard and the business end of Holiday Pies myself. I've tried for years, and I've failed." He bounces his cup of coffee over the table as if adding an exclamation point.

I can't believe my brother just threw me under the bus like that. Not once has he come to me asking for help. And he waits until now to tell us he's been saddled with Holiday Pies? If I remember right, he said he would gladly take over the family business. I'll have to remind him of that later. No use in causing a scene in here any more than we already are.

Dad and Mom exchange a brief glance before Dad clears his throat. "I'll come out of retirement. It's the only right thing to do."

Mom gives a stoic nod. "And I'll get back to pounding the pavement like I used to do in the beginning. I'll rustle up as many new vendors as possible, and I'll do it all by Christmas. You'll see. We'll double the orders, and I'll have that factory bustling far more than it ever has before."

Tanner pinches his eyes shut a moment as if he's at wits' end with my parents' meager declaration of support. "The factory is running at capacity. I don't think we could move any faster if we tried." He offers a sorrowful look my father's way. "And with your back, I think you might be more of a risk than an asset to the farm. No offense. I could always use your keen eye, though, if you ever want to drive around the property in a golf cart."

Dad concedes with a grimace. "Come spring, you won't be able to stop me."

Tanner looks over at me, and for the first time I feel the weight of my brother's frustrations, the heft of the burden riding over his back. A horrible feeling of guilt washes over me, coating me on the inside, thick with regret and remorse. While I've been living the high life, he's been breaking a sweat, breaking his back just to keep the cogs in the wheel churning.

"I'll step up." I hear myself say.

The entire table freezes solid as if I just offered to nuke the building.

Tanner huffs a dull laugh, those tired eyes still pinned to mine. "That'll be the day."

"And that day is today. I'm ready to roll my sleeves up and see what we've got. I'm sure I can make this work." It feels invigorating to know I can dig my claws into the business and pump some life back into it. I'm sure I can.

"I knew it!" Mom bleats so loud half the café turns our way. She lunges at me with a tight embrace. "It's Graham to the rescue. I can always count on you, son." Her phone pings, and she pulls it forward. "Oh, dear. It's Caroline down at the shop. She thinks the water main under the bathroom is about to burst."

Dad lets out a strangled cry of frustration as he gets out of his seat. "When it rains, it pours." He helps my mother up. "Tell her we're on our way, and I'll call a plumber." He shoots a finger my way. "Thank you for stepping in and helping your brother. I know he'll appreciate it no matter how small or large the effort."

They scramble out the door just as a wily redhead makes her way in, shaking the snow from her hair as if it were lice. A hard groan comes from me, and I don't do a thing to hide it. I can't help it. In the short time I've been here, Sabrina Jarrett has set out to make my existence agonizing. To top it off, last night I dreamed I was being chased down by a redheaded hunter wearing spiked stilettos while wielding a razor-sharp umbrella my way.

The urge to shrink in my seat hits me, so I do. "I mean it, man. I want to help," I say quickly to my brother, because knowing how relentless this Sabrina chick is, I only have a matter of seconds left with him.

"Sure you do." He downs the rest of his coffee. "But it's too late. I've already let the managers know the pink slips are coming as soon as Christmas is over."

My stomach sinks as soon as he says *pink slips*. I would never want to be party to letting people go, especially at Christmastime. Even if they are technically losing their jobs after the holidays, I fully understand the fear those people are feeling right about now.

Sabrina lands an icy kiss to my cheek, and I glance to the counter and catch Missy wide-eyed with surprise. I can't help but hide a smile. I'd like to think she were a tad bit jealous.

"Well, look who's here." Sabrina lands between my brother and me as her cloying perfume settles in our midst. "It's a double Holiday surprise." Her eyes slit to my brother a moment before reverting to me. "So, what's on the agenda for today? Apple picking? Pie slinging? You Holidays have always been a barrel of fun."

Missy comes over and lands in the seat to my right, a cheesy grin growing on her face. "Yeah, Graham, what's on the agenda today?" There's a devious look in her eyes, and as much as I want to chuckle, I'm a bit afraid to at the moment. Nothing good ever comes from that look. "A hostile takeover of the entire state of Colorado? A bank heist? Or perhaps just a bite out of the local real estate market? I'm sure you can snap up half of Gingerbread with just the change in your pocket." She nods to Sabrina as if she's marketing me. Wait a minute... I glance from Sabrina to Missy. Didn't Nick mention his little sister was the best matchmaker this side of the Mississippi? I think I know what's going on here. But why on earth would Missy think Sabrina is the right match for me? It makes zero sense. My stomach drops because maybe it does.

Tanner blows out a breath as he looks to me. That weight of the world stare makes me feel like trash, like I've let my little brother down, and I know I have.

"We're going to Cater," he announces. "If you ladies want to join us, you're welcome. It's Take a Tour of the Factory Monday." He tilts his head my way and lifts his cup to me. "Let's see what the golden boy can do. Rumor has it, not every superhero wears a cape."

Missy looks from Tanner to me as her mouth falls open, and I'm sorry she has to be here to witness Tanner's display. But it could be worse. She could take him up on that tour of the factory. They both could.

Sabrina rises to stand and raises her shoulders at Missy. "I hope patent leather boots are the right look for Cater this time of year." She hikes up a heeled hoof before skipping over to the door.

Missy sheds a tiny smile sealed with deviant intent as she looks to my brother and me. "Bring on the pies, boys. I'm ready if you are."

The four of us walk out the door, and just like that, it indeed gets worse.

The drive to Cater is about a good solid half hour with the roads icy as they are. Missy volunteered to drive out with Tanner, and I got stuck with Chatty Cathy who doesn't seem to come with a shut-off switch to save my sanity. I hear all about the trials and temptations as her reign of Miss Corn Shucker three years in a row. It turns out, Sabrina spent some time in the national beauty pageant circuit as well and is considering opening a boutique that caters to young girls who might be looking into that profession. I don't have the heart to tell her it's probably more of a hobby than it is a profession, and that Gingerbread isn't exactly brimming with beauty pageants, save for the one. But I'm not here to burst anyone's bubble. Tanner distributed all the bad news one can handle on a Monday, and I don't plan on adding to anyone's misery.

We come upon the factory, and my stomach drops at the dismal scene. Coming here as a kid, it looked towering and strong, all steel and might—and here it looks woefully small, all rust and fatigue. The paint is peeling away from the side of the building, and the sign that once boasted *Home of Holiday Pies* sits crooked and faded as a memory.

"Geez," I say under my breath as I glide into the parking spot next to Tanner's. I can't remember when I was here last. For as seldom as I've visited Gingerbread, I sure as heck didn't bother to make the trek out to this old place. In my mind, Tanner had it handled. He seemed to be on top of everything—and, come to find out, the weight of it all has all but collapsed on top of him.

We get out and follow Tanner in through the giant delivery door opened in the back with Missy next to him and Sabrina bouncing dutifully by my side. It almost feels as if we've paired off, as if we were couples, and I shake that thought right out of my head. Missy wouldn't be interested in Tanner that way, would she? Nope. Missy is playful and cheery, and Tanner is as serious as an unemployment slip, about as cheery as a root canal.

Sabrina takes ahold of my hand just as Missy turns back and catches the action. That partial grin on her face glides right off before she freely glides in a little closer to my brother. A ripe anger rips through me at the sight. She's not serious, is she? She can't be. This entire day is a bad mind warp. A bad *dream* that I wouldn't mind waking up from.

We step past the tired office that doubles as an employee lounge and into the factory proper. This has always been my favorite part of the facility, the inner workings, where rows and rows of pies descend with elegance on the conveyer belts. I step in deep and take in a lungful of air, just waiting to inhale those warm spices I used to live for and—nothing.

"Where's the fresh smell?" I pause, carefully detangling my hand from Sabrina's. I take a few more steps into the factory and note the machines and pulleys all still humming away as if they were right where I left them. Several employees with hairnets supervise the pies as they drop from the conveyer belts and quickly box them, but there's not one hint of holiday cheer in the air.

"What smell?" Tanner looks miffed as he leads us to the start of operations into the room that houses the fresh apples, cooked pumpkins, and squash.

"You know, the scent, the pumpkin spice that used to knock us off our feet when we were kids."

Tanner scoffs over at me. "Exactly how long has it been since you've been here? Never mind. I think I have a pretty good idea." He looks to Missy and nods. "I had to switch out the spices we used years ago. It was a cost factor."

"Oh, I get it." Missy nods my way. Those eager violet eyes have a touch of sadness in them. "The cost of our ingredients alone is enough to make me want to pass out. That's why I hate giving our food away for free." She casually shoots a look of disdain to Sabrina.

"*Please*"—Sabrina scoffs almost as proficiently as my brother just did—"I'm doing you a favor by hosting all my club meetings at the bakery. Just think how all those women who would have never set foot in that carb factory now have somewhere to purchase all their bakery needs."

Missy scowls my way. "Funny how nary a need has arisen. I'm betting they don't pack a bag of snickerdoodles before they head off to spin class. Not that I have anything against being fit. I myself jog three miles a day when it's not an ankle breaking winter." She turns to me. "Noel will love me in the spring."

"She will." I grin. "And I'll make sure she writes from New York to tell you so."

"Ha!" Missy is quick to laugh in my face. But our eyes latch onto one another for a moment, and for the life of me I can't seem to look away. My heart beats a little faster, and her expression grows serious. If I were to guess, there is something palpable happening here, an attraction that I don't think either one of us can deny. My breathing picks up, and it's as if I'm seeing Missy for the very first time, with new eyes, a new heart.

Tanner gives a solemn applause. "Is the show over? Because I'm ready to start the tour now."

And he does just that. Tanner takes us through each depressing play-by-play of what used to be the happiest place on earth. Now it looks as if the factory is conducting its own funeral, each whir of the tired motors penning its own pathetic eulogy. You can't go ten steps without feeling the despair this place emits like a foul odor. The tour wraps up, and both Missy and Sabrina are offered a piece of fresh baked pumpkin pie—in which Missy indulges. Sabrina just stares at it with disgust as if it were growing limbs in front of her eyes.

Tanner nods me to the side as his features harden, and I'm almost afraid to follow him. If he has a few rough words to share with me, most likely I deserve them.

"Well, golden boy? What's your big solution for this money pit? You got a brainstorm brewing in that million dollar head of yours? Because if you do, everyone in here needs to hear it right about now."

I sink back on my heels as I examine the place with a heavy heart. "Yeah, I've got an idea. Go with plan A. Shut the place down after Christmas. This place is a financial mortuary."

Tanner gives a slow blink as if relieved I finally got the message. Losing this place will be a hard pill to swallow, especially for my mother, but it doesn't seem possible to pull it from the edge. Nope. This place went over the side years ago. A decline like this doesn't happen overnight.

Missy looks my way, her lips quivering as if she might cry, and part of me wants nothing more than to comfort her—for her to comfort me.

And then, just like that, she gives Sabrina a shove in my direction, and I can't help but think Monday just got a little worse. It's not quite Sabrina that's bringing me down, as it is the fact Missy is so determined to prove the two of us are a fit.

I'm not a fit with Sabrina Jarrett and her high-heeled mile a minute self-indulgent monologues. Sabrina wraps her arms around me and purrs at least a half dozen indecent things in my ear while Missy bites down on her lip.

Tanner goes over and they strike up a conversation of their own, and she laughs at whatever it is he just told her. And oddly the happier Missy gets, the more she glows in my brother's presence—the angrier I get, and the more I glower next to Sabrina.

I'm not sure what's happening anymore, what's up and what's down, who I should see and who I should stay away from.

Sabrina tucks a kiss just under my ear, and Missy glances this way in time to see it, her entire face burning like a bright red bow.

Is that a smidge of jealousy I detect?

And just like that, my spirit soars as I drink down the prospect.

There might just be a bright light at the end of this dismal visit, and her name is Mistletoe Winters.

3

Baby it's Cold Outside

Missy

December is always the busiest month of the year for most people, but when you have a thriving business in the heart of downtown Gingerbread, each day flies by like a spinning top. Jenna and Holly are working the front of the bakery while I tirelessly bake batch after batch of as many Christmas cookies as my ovens can handle, and when I'm not doing that, I'm trying to piece together the puzzle that is the Holiday Pie debacle. I've laid out a half a dozen pumpkin and apple pies, each just about ready to head into the oven themselves. But the goal isn't to bake simply a pumpkin pie or an apple. It's to somehow alter the recipe enough so that it miraculously takes the pie to the next level.

"I'm here!" Mom trills as she removes her scarf while skipping through the kitchen. "Holly called and said it was a 911 situation, and I said no worries, Mighty Mom is on her way!" Her ruby red lips expand with her signature grin. Her golden curls look fresh from the beauty parlor, and she's wearing an incredibly cheery bright red sweater. It would be a shame to get even a speck of flour on it. For the most part, my mother looks gorgeous at any given hour, but there's an extra sparkle about her today that I can't quite put my finger on.

"We're fine, Mom, really. Besides, you look far too impeccable to be throwing on a hairnet and apron. In fact, you look like you're ready for church."

"*Ha!*" she balks. "Church? You're such an ageist, Missy. You think that just because a woman of a certain age gets all gussied up, then she must be going to a house of worship." She steals a truffle mouse off the counter and moans as it melts in her mouth. "Mmm, divine, but you really mustn't make your food look like vermin."

"Are you kidding? Those are one of my top ten bestsellers. Everyone who comes in here wants at least a dozen Christmas mice to go." I'm partial to the tiny creatures for several reasons—the cut almond slivers for ears, the red nonpareil eyes, and that eerie shoestring licorice tail—but the real reason they landed on my nice list this year is because they're no-bake. You simply mix chocolate wafer crumbs and melted chocolate chips to form their bodies. No-bake means I don't need to crowd an oven. Whenever I see an employee standing around with nothing to do, I suggest they whip up a batch.

Mom makes a face. "Yes, well, preach it to the choir because I won't be at the evening service tonight." She gives a little wink. "Your father is taking me to Le Roux."

"Le Roux?" I cease from hovering over the bevy of pies as I stalk over to her. "Wow, a fancy French restaurant. No wonder you look like you're about to paint the town red—no pun intended. May I ask what the occasion is? Do I want to know?" With my mother you can never be too sure. Mom and Dad instated date night a few years back when it practically became a buzzword for couples the world over. Anything that involves dressing up and enjoying a good meal will undoubtedly get my mother's attention, and much to the chagrin of my father's wallet, they have indulged religiously in date night without missing a week.

"I sold my very first condo this afternoon!" Her voice hits its upper register as her excitement hits full bloom. "You know, from that complex I scored last week? I have another showing this weekend, and if all goes as planned, I'll have half the units sold before the new year."

"That's fantastic! I say you deserve that dinner. And in light of recent French developments, you may absolutely not assist me in the kitchen this afternoon. I'm fine, I promise. I'm just trying out a few different recipes."

She grunts as she observes the rows of uncooked pies. "They all look the same to me. Six apple, six pumpkin. No offense, but you're going to have to get a little more creative than that." Her lips twist in a bow. "It all looks a little, I don't know, boring."

"It is boring. I think that's the problem. I just can't think of something special enough to wake it up."

"Oh, Missy, you've always been an over-thinker." She pulls an apple pie toward her over the marble countertop and glares at it as if it offended her on some level. "Pop quiz." Her eyes narrow in on mine, and I can't help but groan. Growing up, my mother demanded that my siblings and I wade our way through our problems by dissecting them as if they were problems on a test—the test of life, my mother would say. "What else could you do with an apple to make it tempting and delicious?" She gives an impish grin as if she's already aware of the answer.

My voice hums in my throat for a minute as I try to decipher this. "Caramel apple!"

Her eyes widen as she looks to me. "Very good. And give me something else for this pie." She points to the next plain apple pie staring back at me.

"Salted caramel apple!" My mind explodes with a million ideas at once. "Praline apple crunch, cinnamon apple crisp," I say, pointing to each of the other pies.

Mom nods with approval before yanking over a jiggling pumpkin pie. "These are far easier—you must know something that could make a pumpkin pie sing."

"S'mores!" It comes to me without any effort at all. I guess I have to give Mom and her think-your-way-out-of-your-paper-bag mentality some serious props. I think we're really onto something. "Hazelnut swirl, maple brownie chunk, and, of course, gingerbread." I give a little shrug as she blows me a kiss.

"Well done, Missy! I'll give you an A for creativity." She pulls on a pair of tight black gloves that make her hands look svelte and beautiful. "I'd better head out to meet your father. I'll catch up with you soon, dear! *Toodles!*" She breezes out the door as quick as she came in, and my mouth is rooted to the floor.

"That woman is a genius," I say as Holly comes in, her blonde hair frazzled. Her apron looks as if a dozen chocolate hungry children attacked her all at once. For once I'd like to beat her to the punch and give myself a pop quiz.

"And this place is a circus." She frowns at the pies. "Any luck?"

"Only the best," I say, already whipping around the kitchen to gather the ingredients I need to make all of my Holiday Pies dreams come true.

"Yeah, well, you're going to need it. Guess who's having date number two right in our café?"

I suck in a sharp breath as I peer around the corner. "Oh my goodness!" My face flushes with heat. There they are, Graham Holiday and Sabrina Jarrett enjoying coffee and an entire slew of Christmas cookies—on the house most likely. I can't help but grunt at the sight as Graham bites into a stain glassed window cookie. I stayed late yesterday baking batch after batch. They're some of our top sellers because they're so beautiful to look at. Graham laughs at something Sabrina says, and my stomach sinks. "I guess I did it," I say, breathless.

"Yup." Holly butts her shoulder against mine. "You hijacked two more lives and set them on the trajectory toward alimony and an entire slew of attorneys. They'll never work, and you know it. They're not right for one another. Despite his supernatural success, Graham is down-to-earth, and Sabrina is just a corn shuck princess who lives in a hot pink plastic bubble."

I take a moment to frown over at my sister. She's not usually such a pessimist when it comes to love. I have no idea why she's picking on my potential power couple. Sabrina and Graham are clearly cut out for one another. She's the epitome of vanity, and he has an ego that can hardly squeeze through the door. I'm shocked they haven't eloped by now.

I tap my sister's foot with my own. "But what about our dream of him whisking her away to New York? Think of all the inventory we'll save, the profits we might actually make." My own voice actually sounds pathetic to me. What was meant to be a battle cry came out as more of a whine. It's true, though. With Sabrina and her cohorts out of the picture, we might actually crawl out of the red.

Holly shakes her head with that look of disapproval all over her face. "At the end of the day, money is just a tool. But love, that's something money can't buy." Those insistent eyes of hers assure me I'm making the wrong move.

"Don't look at me like that. What's done is done. Sabrina and Graham are as good as engaged." My body bucks as if I were sobbing.

Sabrina glances our way and does a quick double take. She bounces out of her seat and races to the counter.

Holly gives me a firm shove in that direction. "You're on."

"Sabrina." I press my hands over my apron as I plaster on a smile. "What a pleasant surprise." Shockingly, it doesn't at all sound sarcastic. What is happening to me? "I see things are going well for you." I tip my head over to their table as Graham turns my way and gives an unenthused wave. He doesn't look happy at all, and yet somehow this makes my spirit soar.

"He's antsy," she hisses, her blood red lips quivering as if she were rabid. "He's making every excuse just to leave. What do I do? What do I tell him?" For the first time ever, Sabrina looks as if she's about to crawl out of her skin. I've never seen this unsure, jittery side of her, and a part of me is lapping it up. But this is no time to gloat.

Just great. I line up a great catch, and suddenly Sabrina is short on clues on how to keep him coming back for more.

"I don't know," I hiss right back. "I'm boring, remember?" A thought comes to me. "Wait a second." I glance back to the kitchen at those rows and rows of sweet confections just waiting to come to life, and my heart sinks a bit. "Tell him you have an idea that can help save Holiday Pies." She leans in, and I spill every last salted caramel detail.

Sabrina takes off with a spring in her step and they start in on a casual conversation, which quickly turns lively, and just as they seem to spark to life, I seem to power down. It's as if my insides are coated with lead. A selfish part of me wanted to be the one who saved Holiday Pies, and for the life of me I can't figure out why. It doesn't matter who saves it— merely that it's still operational at the end of the day. People's livelihoods are at stake. I happen to know firsthand that many of the people who work at the factory live right here in Gingerbread. And the last thing Gingerbread needs is for the unemployment rate to increase. Those are my neighbors. They have families, children who will undoubtedly want a long list of presents this Christmas and every one after that, too. Plus, I love the Holidays. I love Graham.

A breath hitches in my throat as I stare right at him. He must sense a disturbance in the force because he turns my way slightly and our eyes hook over one another. Sabrina slaps the side of his arm and gifts me a dirty look in the process, and I shake all thoughts of loving Graham Holiday right out of my head. I spin on my heels and bump into Holly.

"I meant I love his family," I mumble my way past her. My goodness, where is my head? It's clear I'm delirious from staring at baked goods all morning. My mind is turning into dough.

"*What?*" She follows me back to what amounts to the test kitchen of Holiday Pies as I stare at all the potential options that lie ahead. And to think, Sabrina is out there taking all the credit while I roll up my sleeves to break a sweat. "I think all that eggnog you're sipping on the side has gone to your brain."

I shake my head her way. "I'm not in love with Graham." I bite down so hard over my bottom lip, I'm positive it's about to split. I try my best to refocus my thoughts as I study the neat rows of pies, each awaiting their final culinary destiny.

"Newsflash, sister"—Holly folds her arms across her chest as if she's had it with me—"we have about six dozen more gingerbread houses we need constructed and delivered to customers who have already *paid* for their orders, and you're busy playing matchmaker with more than a few pie ingredients?" Her affect softens, and the moisture builds in her eyes. Holly has been a lifelong crier. She *earned* the nickname Crybaby. It was just a fact I was spouting when I called her it all those many years ago. But at the moment, she's making me want to boo-hoo right along with her.

"It's not what you think." I shake my head, trying my best to uphold my argument, but my chest feels as if a mountain is sitting on it. "I was just talking to Sabrina and—"

She cuts me off. "You realized you made a mistake."

I try my hardest to refute her, but I can't seem to move past the boulder sitting in my throat.

My lips press together. "That's not what I was going to say."

"You didn't have to. Your subconscious did it for you." A self-satisfied smirk comes to her face as she turns to leave abruptly. "Don't worry. I'll spy on the faux lovebirds while you hide out in the kitchen." She pauses before she heads out of sight. "Good luck with those pies. I already know they'll turn out great. You're pouring your whole broken heart into them."

"You're such a sap!" I shout after her, spiking my fists into my hips as I grunt out at the legion of pies I've set out to tackle. Holly is right. I don't have time to play superhero. I have a business to run—an entire village of gingerbread houses to build. But as much as my feet want to turn in another direction, my heart says *finish this first*.

So I do. I bake a dozen designer pies as a test run of what I'm hoping will be delicious things to come, and I do it all for Graham Holiday, but I will never tell a soul—not Holly, not Sabrina, and certainly not Graham himself. There are some acts of kindness best kept to yourself.

I mix and melt, adding ingredient after ingredient, taking the brilliant suggestions my mother prodded me toward to the very next level. No thought is too wild, no idea too out of reach to strive for. It's as if everything I had was riding on these very pies—as if it were my neck on the line, my final paycheck looming up ahead. At the end of the day, those factory workers, the *Holidays* are family. They need this more than anyone on this planet needs a gingerbread house delivered today. One by one I set them in the oven and the kitchen lights up with their delicious scents, and something in me comes alive with each hint of something new. While they're baking, I peer into the café and note that Sabrina and Graham are still chitchatting away, their intermittent laughter seems to be set on a regular timer, and my heart sinks clear to middle earth. It wouldn't matter even if I did have feelings for Graham. It's becoming clearer with every cookie they gobble down that Graham Holiday is a very taken man.

On Friday, after an arduous workweek, after three more days of witnessing the atrocity-slash-quasi-blessing in disguise that is Sabrina and Graham's blossoming relationship, I finally arrive home—correction, I arrive at Graham's to pick up Noel.

"Knock, knock," I say unenthusiastically. It's my usual spiel, but it's been far more cheerier than anything I can muster right now. Typically, Graham and I exchange a few lighthearted barbs before Noel and I go on our merry way, but I don't even have the energy for a single wayward word from that man. It's all wearing on me, the gingerbread house hustle and bustle, the snarky comments from Holly about the biggest mistake I've ever made in my life—to hear her say it, you'd think I gave an entire gaggle of children to a complete stranger—and, of course, Graham himself. Yes, his presence is finally eroding me on the inside. Now that's something I'll freely admit.

The door swings open, and there he is, larger than life. His dark hair is slicked back, and his dimples are ironically neatly in place and doing what they do best, dimpling at me. He's wearing his long dark winter coat, and those rugged boots I find so alarmingly attractive on him are still firmly on his feet. The warm scent of his cologne feels like a titillating invitation, and I blush just thinking about it. I hate that my biological response to him overrides my need to detest him properly.

"Heading out on a hot date with Sabrina?" I can't even muster the energy to frame that properly with sarcasm. It sounded more like a pathetic fact, and pathetically, it probably is. That is what I wanted, isn't it?

He takes a step down the porch and locks the house up behind him before turning back to me with a grin.

"*You* would actually be the girl of the hour. Noel's still at the lot. Why don't you come with me? Rumor has it, you still don't have a tree up."

I make a face, but something inside me purrs at the thought of being the girl of the hour. "I don't have a tree for the same reason you don't have a tree. Noel will chew it to matchsticks by morning. She's already barreled through my closet, and I don't have a single set of matching high heels left. And purses? She ate the Coach purse my mother gifted me last Christmas. All of it—*gone*. And don't get me started on what she does with the laundry she gets ahold of. I'm going to need a whole new wardrobe once she gets out of puppyhood. By the way—how long does puppyhood last, anyway? Six weeks? Seven?" I'm secretly hoping for less.

Graham tips his head back and belts out a laugh. Just the sight of this beautiful man with a smile on his face sends my heart thumping a little too fast.

"Try two years." His lids hood low as he looks to me, and my stomach bursts with heat. "But it's nothing you'll need to worry about. I've got a whole closet of Italian leather waiting for her back in Manhattan. Your shoes will be safe soon enough."

"You wish," I say as we head to his truck, and I pile myself inside.

The engine roars to life, and we head out toward the tree lot. It's nice like this with Graham, a spate of silence while watching the evergreens painted with snow as they melt by in a blur. I've always secretly felt that Gingerbread is one of the most romantic settings in the world. I might be a great matchmaker, but I've always known Gingerbread has played a big role in each and every love story that's ever unfolded here. It's simply magical here. Gingerbread spells love out with the crisp clean air, the powdered sugar covered trees, the beauty of its sparkling blue lake.

The tree lot is just around the bend, and my insides twist at the thought of what little help I've been to my brother.

"A part of me dreads seeing Nick." I glance to Graham as the streetlights wash him an ethereal blue. Even in this strange light, Graham is unnaturally gorgeous. It's a wonder there's not an entire mob of Gingerbread women beating down his door. But I guess if Sabrina is his official plus one, she's put the word out on the street that he's forever off-limits. Once Sabrina decides she wants something, either fate or her daddy makes sure she gets it. I'm beginning to think they're one in the same.

"Why's that? You owe him money?" He gives a quick wink my way.

"No, it's nothing like that. I just feel like I'm slacking off as far as putting in time at the lot this year. I'm usually a regular, and this year I'm more of a ghost of Christmas past." And with all the responsibility at the bakery, I'll most likely never be a regular at the tree lot again.

"Ghost of Christmas past. Clever. I see what you did there." He takes in a breath, and I can't help but note the fact his chest looks expansively enormous. Graham must live at the gym back home. I don't remember him being so stunningly fit. It's as if he turned into this beefcake of a man while I wasn't looking. His body has always been fit and lean, but nothing like this. Graham Holiday has never played fair. "But I wouldn't worry about it. You're busy. You've got a life of your own. We've got a kid now for Pete's sake." He glances my way and blesses me with that killer grin for a moment.

"Yeah, a kid that Nick is watching most of the time." It's as if I'm determined to make myself feel bad today. It's true, though. I miss Noel fiercely while I'm doing time at the bakery. A part of me wants to ask Graham to bring her down a couple times a day just so I can get a quick squeeze in, but another, wiser part of me knows that too much Graham Holiday wouldn't be a good thing. It's bad enough I'm spending far too much time with him as it is. The more time I spend with him, the more I dislike Sabrina.

"Don't feel bad over that. Nick has practically begged me to leave Noel with him for a few hours each day, if not longer. She's a hit with the kids, the reindeer have adopted her as one of their own, and she sells more trees than all the employees combined. I'm about to start charging him. So if he gives you a hard time, remind him that you're doing him a favor."

A tiny laugh brews in my chest as we pull into the lot. "I will. Don't tell Savanah, but I think Noel is vying for the role of favorite niece as far as my brother goes."

We share a quick laugh as we head out into the bitter cold. The sun—or more to the point, the idea of the sun—just set, and the sky is that strange violet shade of gray that I love so much on a cold winter's night. It always feels magical to look up to see a purple velvet sky, and for some reason, tonight's sky, peppered with its crushed diamond stars, looks far more magical than any of the others.

"Wow," I gasp as I stare straight up. "Now that's a beautiful sight."

"I couldn't agree more," he whispers it low and husky, and when I glance down, I find it's me Graham is staring at. My cheeks heat far hotter than any of those stars, and I do the only thing I can think of—walk right past him.

The lot is lush with trees and brimming with people milling around with hot cocoa and cookies as they inspect each tree as a prospect to decorate their home with. We spot Nick near the cash register, and I bravely head straight for him.

Nick glances up just as he closes out an order and steps over with that affable smile he's famous for. My favorite attribute of my brother's personality has always been his easygoing attitude, but my guilt still has me standing on edge.

"I'm so sorry I haven't been here to help with the lot!" I blurt as if the confession were necessary, and judging by how light I suddenly feel, it's apparent it was. "I feel terrible knowing you needed me, and I couldn't be here. Please don't be angry." I lunge at my brother with a hug and note the fact he holds the scent of a very ripe evergreen. He hugs me right back, and I pull away to assess the damage, but he doesn't look upset in the least.

"Why would I be angry? Holly and Tom just brought Savanah by and picked out a tree. She told me about all those pies you baked this week. And then you donated them to the homeless shelter? Are you gunning for citizen of the year? Because I'm up for that, too, you know." He offers a mock sock to my arm and laughs. "Don't sweat a thing, sis. I know you're pulling out your hair this time of year at the bakery. Whatever you need, I'm here for you."

"Great." Graham rolls back on his heels, a smug smile cresting his lips. "She needs a tree. Tonight's the night it's getting done."

Nick glances at his old friend up and down for a moment. "Make sure the tree is the only thing that's getting done. What are the two of you thinking, sharing a dog?" He casts a look my way that suggests I should know better. For as much as Holly would like to see Graham and me together, I'm pretty sure my brother would love for us to be twelve states apart at any given time. And I happen to share his sentiment. My insides cinch at the thought, and for the life of me I can't figure out why. "One of you is going to be on the losing end of that deal." He gives Nick a light shove to the chest. "And it better not be my sister."

"It will be." Graham doesn't miss a beat with those dimples of his still digging in deep. "Come on, Sprig." He waves me over as we head to the forest of trees just behind the tent. "Let's make it a big one. It's on him!"

Nick ticks his head for me to follow, and I do.

"*Hey*—where's Noel?" I ask, struggling to keep up with them.

"I've got the guys in charge of the reindeer keeping an eye on her. She'll be fine." Nick nods to the bevy of evergreens in our way. "Get a good one. Last time I'm floating you a freebie."

"Ha! You wish!" A laugh bounces in my chest, and I huff and puff my way into the powdery night and find Graham out by the fifteen footers. "Hey—nitwit! Some of us don't have a vaulted ceiling!" I cry with glee as I scoop up a handful of snow and pelt him with it.

"Who are you calling a nitwit?" He pelts a snow bomb my way, and it splatters over my shoulder. A fireball of laughter erupts from my throat, and suddenly I feel sixteen again, doing exactly this with exactly him. Graham and I have had more than our fair share of snowball fights growing up. Long after everyone else gave up, the two of us would carry on for hours. It was as exhausting as it was exhilarating.

"I'm only repeating what I heard your mother say about you." I scoop up a pile of snow, and before I can form a proper sphere, he has an entire arsenal of snow globes ready to detonate freely over my person. "Don't you dare!" I run screaming and laughing into the woods where the lights from the tree lot fade to shadows and that velvet night sky seems to stretch down and kiss the snowy ground.

Graham pelts me over the back, and I belt out a shrieking laugh that curls up into the heavens. I head for a pile of snow just behind the lot and throw my hands in the air, exhausted. It's quickly becoming clear I'm not sixteen anymore. This body is ready to surrender defeat, and I haven't even pegged him properly in the face.

"I give! Uncle!" I shout, collapsing in the fluffy white mass before turning over and flailing my limbs in and out in an attempt to make a snow angel.

Graham falls next to me and pulls me onto his lap before shoving what amounts to a snow pie right in my face.

"*ARRGGHH!*" I let out a cry that goes on for days. "Do you always have to have the last word? Last *misdeed*?" I ask as I do my best to wipe myself clean before my eyelids freeze shut. That was a classic Graham Holiday move, and I should have seen it coming the second he pulled me over. What did I think he was going to do? Cradle me with romantic intentions? I'm pretty sure he's saving all the romantic moves for Sabrina, and my blood begins to boil—over the pie in the face, not Sabrina. I'm not angry over the fact he wants to cuddle with Sabrina, am I?

"Why no, I don't have to have the last word." He laughs at the thought, and his chest bucks beneath me. "More like the last pie in the face." His dimples dig in as our eyes hook to one another. "What's this about you mass producing pies and then donating to the homeless shelter? You trying to singlehandedly give Holiday Pies a bad rap?" He gives my side a light tweak, and it's only then I realize I'm still sitting on his lap. And seeing that the frozen ground is my only other option, I'm clearly staying put.

"Not a bad rap." A ragged breath runs through me. "Just a fair shake at life." A part of me is begging to spill the truth, but Sabrina's face keeps popping up in the back of my mind, threatening me not to do it.

Graham winces a moment. "It's okay. I know all about it."

"You do?" Something in me loosens. I never intended to keep this a secret from him. Who cares whose idea it was? I'm so excited about the designer pies that I want to divulge every delicious ingredient to him.

"Yes." He pulls me in a little closer, and his minty breath washes over my cheek. "Sabrina told me all about it. She said she had a brainstorm, and she asked you to test out at least a dozen pies in ways no one in my family would have thought up in a million years. That was really nice of you, Sprig." He bounces me over his knee as if I were a three-year-old. "I owe you one for that."

A dull laugh rattles within me, and that mountain is right back to sitting on my chest. "It sounds like you owe Sabrina one." I bite down on my bottom lip to keep from telling the truth. I can feel it percolating right beneath the surface, ready to spew out at the slightest nudging in that direction.

He grimaces at the thought, and yet those dimples flirt with me mercilessly. "I thanked her right away. I think that's plenty." He winces. "But I'm pretty sure she's looking for a monetary payout."

"Money is her middle name," I whisper as I do my best to push Sabrina out of the picture for a moment.

My heart grows heavy as I drink down his features. Graham Holiday has my adrenaline hitting its zenith just being in this close proximity. It's almost alarming the way he's that much more comely once you get within kissing range. Not that I'm going to kiss him. He's practically an engaged man.

I clear my throat. "I'm sure you'll think of something of value to gift her. I hear she's partial to diamonds. Big ones. So get your wallet ready."

A dark laugh rumbles from him, but Graham's eyes never leave mine. "Fat chance on that happening anytime soon."

"So you like playing hard to get. You do realize that will only motivate her." It's true. If anyone likes a challenge, it's Sabrina Jarrett. She's competitive to a fault, and she lives to play dirty. My stomach does a revolution at the thought.

He gives a slow blink. "I guess we have that in common."

I reach down, readying to serve up a piece of snow pie myself when Graham catches my wrist. His gaze remains pinned on mine as his hand glides down and he threads our fingers together instead. It feels nice like this, holding Graham's strong, warm hand, his flesh heating mine to furnace levels. My heart races up my throat as if trying to pop right out of my mouth to have a look around at the commotion for itself. I've never felt so alarmed by my emotions, by the fact my body is responding to another human being so volatilely.

The hint of a smile curls on his lips as his lids hang seductively low. Graham leans in as if he were about to brush his mouth over mine, and if he does, I don't plan on stopping him. In fact, I'd brush mine over his just to soak in how soft his lips are. I lean in, just a breath more, then turn my face and my lips smack him over the cheek. And just like that, Sabrina pops in my head.

"Oh my God." I back away abruptly. "I'm so sorry." I clear my throat as I struggle to my feet, and he bounces up beside me as if he were on springs. "I must have tipped over."

He gives a slow, sad nod as if deciding to play along with the lie. "And I helped keep you upright."

"Yes." It comes out lower than a whisper. "Thank you for that." My heart thumps wild as if it wanted a replay of the moment that almost led to something spectacular.

Nick calls my name in the distance, and the two of us make our way back to the tree lot. We pick out a bruiser of a tree, a seven footer that's as round as it is tall, and Nick helps hoist it in the back of Graham's truck. We collect Noel, and Nick helps me wrap her in a blanket once we get in the cab. I hold her like a baby all the way home, and strangely enough, it feels as if we're an official family—a broken family living in two homes, but nevertheless something about this feels right.

As soon as we get back to my place, Graham gets to the arduous task of landing the gargantuan pine in the tree stand I use year after year. It belonged to my grandparents and somehow made its way to me. It's steel with a wreath forged into it, and I love the fact that every tree I will ever own will sit in the same spot all of my grandparents' trees once sat. I help Graham stage it just right in front of the bay window in the living room, so that when I decorate it to the nines, the neighbors and dog walkers will be able to enjoy it. That's half the fun for me—sharing its beauty with the world. I pull out a box of lights from the hall, and Graham and I string them up in record time. Once we're through, we share a high five and glance over to find Noel curled up by the fire in her cozy dog bed, already snoring away.

"I guess I won't know until morning what she thinks of it." I look back to the tree lit up in a rainbow of pinks and blues, yellows and greens, purple as that night sky tonight, and I can't help but fall in love with this beautiful spruce. But my gaze can't seem to stay on that tree. Instead, I look to Graham, at how impeccably gorgeous he is next to the glorified evergreen, with the fire roaring behind him. Graham Holiday looks resplendent tonight. He outshined that night sky. He makes the tree look like a plain fallen bough. My heart brims as it starts in on that erratic tempo once again like it did at the tree lot.

Graham's sky blue eyes hook to mine, and I can feel him drinking me down.

"So, what about you?" My voice pitches a moment. "Have you and Sabrina put your tree up yet? I mean, you got to admit, the raging fire, the magic of Christmas lights, nothing beats the fresh scent of pine. It's all pretty romantic." My chest bucks when I say that last part. In no way do I want to think about Graham getting romantic with Sabrina Jarrett. Not when I can still feel the stubble on his cheek over my lips. Even if that kiss was accidental, it has clearly left an impression on me.

Graham winces. "I have a confession to make," he whispers. "I'm not in the least bit interested in Sabrina."

My eyes widen at the thought. My heart begins to race as my adrenaline soars. "You're not?" It's all I could muster. A small part of me is very worried what the ramifications of such a confession might mean—for both Sabrina and *me*.

He shakes his head. "You still sorry about that kiss back there? When I'm kissed, I usually like to kiss back."

"Oh"—my fingers touch over my lips a moment—"I thought we were calling it a rescue mission." I bite down on a smile that demands to surface. "I was feeling tipsy, remember?"

His brows dip a notch, and my stomach dips right along with them. Graham is achingly gorgeous, and every last part of me demands to let him know that.

An enveloping heat sears through me as I clear my throat a moment. "So, you're really not into her, huh?"

He shakes his head just enough for me to see it.

"Well, if that's the case, maybe one more kiss wouldn't hurt." I point up, and he drags his eyes from mine for less than a second. "Mistletoe."

"What do you know?" he whispers. "Mistletoe just so happens to be my favorite."

Graham leans in, his lids hooding dangerously low as his fingers dig into the back of my hair. His mouth falls over mine with the slightest brush of the lips, then quickly comes in again for something far more serious. I wrap my arms around him as we fuse our mouths together, our kisses growing far more fevered and lingering by the moment.

My heart detonates in my chest one riotous wallop at a time as if every beat was working up to this incredible moment. Graham kisses me passionately, deeply, in a way that I have never been kissed before, and it's as if a veil pulls back and the blinders fall off and I can see the truth plain as day.

I'm in love with Graham Holiday, and I have been all along.

Graham

I can't get rid of this goofy grin on my face. Missy and I made out like a couple of teenagers last night right up until Noel woke up and began chasing her tail all over the house. We finally decided to pen her in the laundry room. Missy had a doggie gate she bought for that very purpose, and Noel calmed down and went right back to sleep on that overstuffed cushion Missy wedged in there with her. The thing was the size of a Volkswagen, but Missy insisted she wants nothing but the best for her baby girl. Our baby girl, I corrected.

A laugh strums from me at the memory as I head into the Gingerbread Bakery and Café with a single lavender rose in hand. I just dropped Noel off at the lot, stopped off at the florist for something simple. I'd give Missy a dozen of these if I didn't think it'd send us ten paces backward. Nope. Missy is skittish. She's always held her guard up way too high, and I'd hate to have her think I was merely in it to scale the wall. That's not what this is about. That's not what those kisses were about either. I can scale just about any wall I wanted back in New York—heck, probably here in Gingerbread, too, but what Missy and I shared last night was special. I've never had a single kiss that ever made me feel the way she did. I'm not quite sure that I get what's happening here, but the rose seemed like the right move, a thank you and an apology for overstepping my bounds all in one.

No sooner do I step inside and spot Missy pouring a cup of coffee at the counter than a body tackles me with a violent embrace.

I pull back to find Sabrina Can't-Shake-Her-Loose-Jarrett coming at me again, only this time she smacks her lips right over mine.

My insides twist into a knot as I quickly pull away. Like a reflex, my eyes immediately dart to Missy. But she's turned abruptly away, helping the next customer on deck with a shoulder lifted high in our direction as if to shield her from witnessing any more of the spectacle. She has to know that I didn't initiate it, that I would never even contemplate kissing Sabrina, let alone doing it to her face in her shop. My heart feels heavy as that granite slab Missy has her hands pressed against. If I didn't know better, I'd think she were forcing her fingers to remain there rather than wrap themselves around Sabrina's neck—or worse, mine.

"It's beautiful!" Sabrina shrieks as she plucks the rose right out of my hands and spins around, waving it through the air, causing a scene with it in true Sabrina fashion. "Can you believe it?" she sings to someone to her left, and my heart thuds once again as I spot Mom and Dad watching the two of us with bewildered expressions. I'm slow to glance back Missy's way, but, sure enough, she's giggling right alongside Holly. I'm guessing she's figured out the rose was meant for her. Great. And now she gets to watch me squirm my way out of an early morning gathering that I want no part in. "It looks like we are definitely on the right path." Sabrina navigates us to my parents' table, plucks a chair out, and pushes me in it before taking a seat to my right. Both Mom and Dad lift a curious brow my way.

"*Son*." Dad forces a smile to come and go. "Sabrina here tells us you're quite serious. And so soon upon your arrival. How—*interesting*."

Sabrina is quick to wave him off. "Like I always say, why put off a good thing?"

Mom nods as if affirming this madness. "That's what I always say, too." She offers a stern glance in my direction. "Why didn't you tell us this brilliant girl came up with a plan to save Holiday Pies all by her lonesome?"

I can't help but frown as I glance past her at Missy who's busy pretending to organize her platters. She knows perfectly well she's positioned within earshot. A dark laugh lives and dies in my chest. Maybe I should give her a show?

"That's right." I do my best to project my voice. "Sabrina here thought of it all on her own. In fact, she convinced Missy to lend her the kitchen and then proceeded to bake her heart out and donate all the pies she auditioned for us to the homeless shelter downtown." My lips press tight to keep from grinning like some deranged loon. I don't know where to look first. It's like Christmas.

I glance to Missy who's busy rolling her eyes to the ceiling before shooting me a look and heading to the kitchen. I knew she'd catch on quick. I'm slower to cast a glance in Sabrina's direction—but, rather than being angry with the half-truths I've just spouted, she looks mildly confused as she nods in acceptance of this accolade.

"My goodness, Sabrina!" Mom chirps at the benevolence of it all. "The next time I see your father I'll be sure to tell him what an angel he's got on his hands."

More like a devil, but that might be a little harsh. Sabrina did come up with a great idea. And I can't hold the fact she's wildly attracted to me against her. Heck, at this point, I should probably come with my own addiction warning. I can't help but stifle a laugh at how ridiculous that sounds. I would have given anything to have shared that with Missy. I know she'd have a feast with that one. I'm teasing, of course. Sabrina is stalker material no matter how brilliant a scheme she devised to save Holiday Pies.

Sabrina chortles up a storm. "Please do. He's forever looking to hear good things about me. I'm his only child, so it's a direct reflection on how I was raised. My mother and father both worked hard to give me everything I have."

This coming from a twenty-six-year-old woman who still lives at home and has no problem running up her father's credit cards. I know all about the lifestyle she's living because she's told me so in arduous detail. I shoot a quick glance to Missy who is now unnaturally immersed in rearranging cupcakes on a stand, bouncing them around from one place to the next as if it were a game of checkers. Her eyes flit over to mine, and an undeniable spark jumps from her to me. It's powerful, electric, and it is nothing I will ever feel for the girl to my right, currently informing my parents that we will most likely be bicoastal.

Mercifully, Dad has a dental appointment that's due to take place in the next ten minutes, and Mom is quick to usher the two of them out the door. I take advantage of the natural pause by excusing myself for a moment and head over to Missy.

Her lavender gaze matches those petals I purchased, the very ones that found themselves in the wrong hands. I had the entire exchange set up in my mind—me giving Missy the rose—her tearing up with gratitude and then maybe even gifting me another one of those sweet kisses right here in the bakery. Sweetest things going are Mistletoe Winters' lips. That's for sure.

I lean in to whisper, my eyes still magnetically pinned to hers. "Meet me behind the bakery in five minutes?"

She bites down on her bottom lip a moment, and she glances to Sabrina as if she were afraid of her.

"Make it ten." She wrinkles her nose. "You're not getting away that easily." She disappears in the back, leaving her perfume to linger, wrapping itself around me like a scarf I never want to take off. I take in a deep lungful of the sugary scent before heading back to the table and find Sabrina on her feet, gathering her purse.

"There's a boutique down the street that just got in the most fabulous dresses. The auction is just around the corner, and I don't have a thing to wear. Why don't we spend the afternoon trying on some of the more revealing numbers?" Her voice is thick and husky as she leans in with suggestive intent.

"I would, but I don't think they have my size." I pat my thighs. "I'm cut funny."

She twitches her cheek. "Fine. I'll pick out a few extra dresses while I'm at it, though. One for the auction." Her finger glides over my jaw. "One for Christmas Day." She caresses my cheek, and I flinch. "One for New Year's *Eve*." Her thumb rubs over my lips with a hint of promise. "And one sultry number I wouldn't dare wear out of the house in this kind of weather." A throaty laugh bubbles from her. "In fact, I can model that one for you first. Say this weekend sometime? I'm free Saturday night. It would give us something incredible to look forward to." She wets her lips as if she were chomping at the bit—and I do believe she is chomping at the bit.

"Actually, I have a thing"—quick, come up with any *thing*—"with the dog, you know." Thank God for Noel. And now I know how relieved parents the world over must be when they can use their child as an excuse to get out of just about any unwanted event. I guess children—or in this case pet children—really are a blessing in disguise.

"*Ugh.*" She bucks as if she might actually be sick and tosses that rose to the table as if it were diseased. "I've got an idea for you. Get rid of that *thing.*" She hacks out a laugh at her own bad joke as she speeds for the door. "I'd better get going before those divas from my book club swoop in and steal all the good stuff. It's a good thing you're not going. I'd hate to have one of those alley cats try to sink their claws into you. They can't be trusted, you know." She points behind me a moment. "Stay here and hang out with that one all day. She couldn't steal you away from me if she tried!" She blows me an air kiss, and I pretend to catch it. "Ta-ta for now!"

Missy glides in next to me, and together we watch as Sabrina struts down the street in those sky-high heels.

"That looked brutal. And you're right. The two of you don't look serious at all." She gives a playful frown my way.

"First—we're not serious." I wince because on second thought I should never have pretended to catch her kisses. "And second—I was given strict orders to spend the day with you." I pick up the rose off the table and offer it to her with a playful twitch of the brows. I can't imagine she'd accept it after it was so brutally defiled.

"Sorry. I don't do secondhand roses."

"Ah." I toss it back to the table. "I didn't expect otherwise."

"Strict orders, huh?" She tilts her head as she continues to bear those violet eyes into mine. I've dreamed a thousand dreams about those eyes while I've been in New York, and now I know why. I've missed them. More than that, I've needed to see them live and in person. "Maybe I should take the afternoon off. I'd hate for you to get in trouble with your girlfriend."

"*Ooh.*" I slap my chest and whine as if she just shot me. "Maybe you should." I drape my arm around her shoulders. "I just might show you a good time yet."

And that's exactly what I plan on doing—showing Missy a darn good time right here in Gingerbread.

"Where to?" I ask as we hit the frozen air just outside of the bakery. The sky is dark and heavy, but Main Street looks cheery and bright with its festive décor. Ropes of garland decorate every streetlight, every stop sign—and a cheerful wreath hangs in every window and door as far as the eye can see, each one punctuated with a bright red bow. When

Tanner and I were kids, our favorite thing to do was to come down here just before Christmas and listen to the carolers at night. That's something I'd love to do with Missy, maybe bring Noel with us, too. "You got the afternoon off. You're the boss."

She bites down on a smile as her eyes light up. "I do like being the boss." She takes up my hand and begins racing us up the street, but my full attention is on the fact her warm fingers are holding tight to mine. "The hospital has a donation box for the children's unit each year. Santa comes to their unit Christmas morning and distributes all of the presents. It's a really big deal. I like to do my part and add to the magic." She stops in front of Peabody's Bookstore. Her entire countenance glows as she pants through a smile. "What better gift to give than books?"

All of those memories of picking Missy up from the library, meeting her there to sift through the stacks come rushing back. Missy has been a bookworm for as long as I have known her. One year, Nick asked what she wanted from him for Christmas, and she said books—young adult mysteries, I believe were the order of the day. So I'm not surprised in the least Missy believes that books are still the best gift going. My lips curl to the side at the thought.

"What better gift to give than books, indeed," I say as I hold the heavy glass door open for her. Missy strides right in, and I take a moment to enjoy the vanilla sweetness she leaves in her wake.

Peabody's Bookstore has been a staple in Gingerbread far longer than I have—than either of us has been. Inside, the thick scent of paperbacks takes me back to a simpler time, a time when I didn't have to worry about sales reports, deals falling through, or trying to upsell a building that should have been condemned to begin with. I give a sigh of relief as I take a look around the colorful establishment. Rows and rows of shiny new books abound in every direction, each one just waiting to find its reader. The display in the center of the store is a Christmas tree comprised solely of books that stretches to the ceiling. It's an architectural feat on a micro level, and judging by the wonder on Missy's face, I can tell she'd love a tree just like this one in her own home. Now that's something I'd love to make happen for her someday.

"Don't you just love it here? I mean, who wouldn't love to run wild in this place and scoop up all the delicious books they can carry? Reading isn't only good for the mind, it settles your spirit in a way like nothing else can. How else could you possibly travel the world, travel *time*, live a thousand lives—all without leaving the comfort of your home? My perfect day consists of eating and reading next to a cozy fire. Can you imagine if that's all there was to do in life?" She groans as if she yearns for that day with everything in her. "And no matter how old I get, I still have a place in my heart for picture books." She pulls me in by the arm and squeals as she leads us to the children's section—rife with holiday pop-ups, board books, chapter books with cartoon covers, and a rainbow painted bright over the wall. "Since I'm a bookworm by nature, I figure it's never too early to get a kid reading."

"I do love it here," I say, thumping a book called *Oodles of Purple Noodles*. It sounds like something I would have loved as a kid—especially if I happened to be stuck in the hospital. Missy has a heart of solid gold, and as much as it warms me, it makes me proud to see her as the generous woman she's grown up to be. "And I couldn't agree more. I'm a bookworm by nature, too."

"No, you're not." She looks up at me, disbelieving. "You're forgetting we have a long, and dare I say, annoying history together. I know you too well to believe you." Missy starts right in on snapping up book after book.

"I'm not kidding. Reading's been a hobby of mine for as long as I can remember. My mother got me started by bringing me right here to this very bookstore. I don't think I'd be who I am today without spending copious amounts of time combing the aisles of Peabody's."

Missy stops short and frowns over at me, her left brow hiked up on one side. "You wouldn't be who you are today?" she tosses my own words back at me with her mouth agape.

"So the moral of this cautionary tale is that I should probably put these books back."

I bark out a laugh. "What's so bad about me? You're not afraid of a little success, are you?"

"Are you kidding?" Her eyes grow twice their size, and my stomach squeezes tight. Missy is the most beautiful woman I have ever laid eyes on. My heart starts hammering, my adrenaline races through my veins, and I want nothing more than to kiss her right here in the middle of a display that expounds the differences of elves and trolls. And speaking of kisses, those soulful exchanges that happened last night are quickly becoming the elephant in the room. I'd love to bring it up, but for the life of me I can't figure out how.

Missy hands me the stack of books in her arms, and I marvel at their heft a moment. This seemingly innocent pile easily weighs twenty pounds.

"Graham, let me be the first to tell you that you didn't have a little success." She shakes her head my way. "You are living the dream. You left Gingerbread and hit the jackpot in New York City of all places. I'm surprised they haven't done a write-up of you in the paper."

I wince a moment before confessing, "They may have called, and I may have forgotten to get back to them."

"Ah-ha!" She arches a brow. "Well, at least you're hard to get in *some* capacity." She speeds past me as she snaps up picture book after picture book.

"Whoa." I take off, struggling to catch up with her. "Was that a dig at my friendly nature?" My chest bounces with a silent chuckle. "You would be right, though. I haven't exactly played the part of recluse for the last few years." A move I'm quickly regretting. I'm pretty sure it's the last thing Missy is looking for, someone with a long history with just about everybody. I know I wouldn't want that for her. My heart thuds hard in my chest because it's becoming increasingly clear that I do want something with her.

She twists those pretty little lips in a bow while kneeling to pick up a stack of felt covered books with the title *The Christmas Puppy and His Magic Bone.*

"Hey, at least you're honest." She pops right back up and drops another load into my arms. "And speaking of honest." Any trace of a smile glides right off her face, and her lips do that quivering thing. My stomach spikes with heat at the sight because I'm terrified she's about to cry. A part of me is wondering if this is when she'll bring up last night. If I've done anything to hurt her, I don't think I could forgive myself. "Sabrina doesn't quite know you're over, does she?"

My eyes close a moment. As relieved as I am that it's just Sabrina she's worried about in truth, I'm a bit worried about that situation myself. "I don't think a skywriter could properly convey the message. But I'll do my best to make it clear."

Missy groans and shakes her head furtively. "Whatever you do, you have to leave me out of it. That woman has a vengeance out for me like no other." Her mouth opens and closes as if she chose to cut loose whatever else was about to bubble from it. "Anyway, I don't really want to talk about Sabrina." She cranes her neck over at the children's book section one last time and gasps before speeding over to the table in the center of the room. "*The Night Before Christmas*!" She wraps her arms around the hardback, cradling it close to her chest, and I can't help but envy the book right about now. "Oh, I love this story *so* much! My mom and dad used to read it to us on Christmas Eve before we went to bed. I'll have to get a few of these for sure. It's the best Christmas book ever!" She hesitates a moment. "Would it be weird if I bought one for myself?" Missy thumbs through the book quickly, moaning and cooing with every turn of the page.

"That part wouldn't be weird, but if you made those noises each time you read it, your neighbors might think you're strange. On second thought, your neighbor already knows that about you." I give a slight wink. "Get the book. We can read it to Noel on Christmas Eve."

Her features soften as she looks to me with those watery lilac eyes. "Really? That's so—*sweet.*" She shakes her head as if it were an impossibility.

"Yes, really. I think Noel needs some quality time with both her parents."

Her lips twitch because she knows it's coming.

"That way"—I start slowly, trying my best to hold back the urge to laugh—"come Christmas morning, she can decide who she wants to live with. You, the woman who dressed her in a Christmas sweater featuring her archenemy—a *cat*—or me, the man with a soothing voice who read her the best Christmas book ever."

She swats me over the arm before adding to the stack I'm holding.

"She'll choose me," Missy says, leading us to the counter out front. "I'm the only soothing voice she's used to. The way you scream the word *no* at her all day, I bet she thinks that's her name."

"It's partially her name. And I can't help it. She's tearing up my rental. I'm pretty sure I owe the Spitzers a new wool rug in the living room."

Missy groans as we head to the cashier, and she pulls out her wallet with the deft and ease of a magician.

"Oh no, you don't." I set the small mountain of books down before whipping out my own wallet. "This one's on me. You're not the only do-gooder around here."

"Graham! No, please don't. You're going to think that's the only reason I dragged you in here." She lifts her credit card to the cashier, and I gently land mine over hers.

"How about this? You let me get the books, and I'll let you get the pizza."

Her lips twist to the side, and I can't help but wish I could taste them one more time.

"Fair enough."

We ante up and lug our load back to Main Street where a sprinkling of snow falls to earth, soft as powdered sugar.

Missy lifts a hand in the air and laughs as her dark curls become dotted with snowflakes. That sight alone takes my breath away.

Missy and I make a mad dash down the street and toss the books into my truck before heading across the street toward Angelino's.

"This way!" Missy takes up my hand, and instead of leading us to the left and into the safe harbor of the establishment that holds the scent of garlic—and is it ever heavenly—we head right, straight toward the fifty-foot pine at the end of Main Street.

Gingerbread adopted the overgrown evergreen about forty years ago as its official Christmas tree, and each year it's strung with lights and oversized ornaments in every size and color. This year is no exception. It's so gray and dark out, regardless of the fact it's merely afternoon, its brilliant white lights glow like a thousand fallen stars. It is most definitely a breathtaking sight, but the tree has nothing on Missy Winters.

My heart wallops in my chest like a shotgun as we duck behind its thick protective branches. Life may be bustling on the other side of this enormous jolly tree, but you would never know it. For all practical purposes, it's just Missy and me, alone in this frozen magical world, and I can't take my eyes off her.

She flashes a quick smile, but her cheeks burn bright as Rudolph's nose as if she were blushing. "I take a selfie in front of the tree every year, and I thought this year maybe you could join me?"

"By all means, Sprig, let's get 'er done." I lean in as she snaps a few pictures, and I toss two of my fingers up over the back of her head.

"Graham Holiday!" She tries to sucker punch me, and I take the opportunity to wrap her arms around me instead. My heart picks up like a jet engine preparing for takeoff, and I can't seem to catch my breath. I steal the moment to wrap my own arms around her as well. "You're really something, you know that?" Her mouth falls open, and I'm half-expecting some quip about my ego, but she doesn't give it.

"You're really something," I whisper. And as much as the old me demands to barb my words, say something caustic that might make her laugh, I can't seem to do it. This isn't the old us. This is the new us, a better version, one I can't seem to stop thinking about. And then it hits me like a freight train in the dark.

I'm in love with Missy Winters.

"You know what?" I tip my head and come shy of winking.

"What?" she whispers, breathless, and I can feel her chest pulsating against mine like a jackrabbit ready to skip over a mountain.

"I think I see mistletoe." My head inches toward hers ever so slightly. I can't help it. I can't seem to help anything about the attraction I feel toward her. It's unavoidable. Missy is beautiful inside and out.

"Where?" She doesn't take those violet eyes off mine.

"Right here." My lips fall over hers, and we exchange a heartfelt kiss that says so much more than words could ever hope to. Missy and I move over one another with long, lingering kisses that electrify the ground we stand on, that send sparks flying straight up to heaven to that magical star that led the wise men to their destinies that holy night so long ago. This right here feels holy and right.

I'm back in Gingerbread, right where I belong, with the girl I've craved for the last five years.

I'm in love with Mistletoe Winters, and it feels like a relief to admit it to myself at last.

4

Making Merry

Missy

"Christmas is in seven days," I lament to Holly as we put together enough sugar cookie trays to feed a small island nation. "SEVEN DAYS!" I howl at the top of my lungs as everyone in the bustling bakery stops cold for less than a second. Every single employee in the shop is wearing the requisite Santa hat with cute little jingle bells attached to the pompom on the end. It's adorable for about ten minutes, but after wearing the earsplitting chime for the better half of eight hours, you begin to hear it in your sleep. I may have attempted to snip them off, but Holly warned me my fingers would be next. She thinks they add that extra layer of holiday cheer. She might be right, but our sanity hangs in the bounds. Cheerful in December—incarcerated in January.

The bakery is beyond busy, with an output of at least thirty gingerbread houses a day. *Thirty.* You would think the closer we got to the big day, the demand for homes built from molasses would dwindle, but that's not the case. The demand actually continues to rise on a steady basis right up until Christmas Eve. Jingle *jingle*!

"Oh, stop it, Missy," Holly hisses as she wraps the oversized platters with cellophane. It's the annual sugar cookie decorating contest at the Boys and Girls Club, and each year Holly and I graciously supply all the undecorated sugar cookies they can handle. Of course, we supply the icing, the non-perils, the sprinkles—which I still like to call jimmies once in a while, the spicy red dots, the chocolate chips, and every conceivable cookie accouterment known to man so that the kids will have the arsenal they need to turn the Boys and Girls Club into an annual mess. But a cheery mess no less.

Jenna comes in and starts lifting the trays right out of Holly's arms. "I'll get these delivered as soon as you girls button them up."

"Thanks!" I call out, trying desperately not to pass out in a pile of golden brown snowmen.

"*So?*" Holly shrugs with that awkward look on her face she gets when she's about to say something salacious. "How are things going with Graham? Anything exciting and X-rated I should know about?"

I can't help but avert my eyes to the ceiling. Holly might be my best friend, but she is also my sister. I have no intent on sharing anything salacious with her ever.

"Holly!" I toss a broken reindeer her way. We have a long-standing tradition of hanging onto the cookies that didn't quite make the cut and feasting on them ourselves—or using them as weaponry as evidenced by my wise decision to do so. "There's absolutely nothing X-rated about the two of us." I give a sly glance around in the event anyone is within earshot. News travels fast in Gingerbread, and I'll be the last person to fuel the gossip train. "We kissed." That's about as much as I would ever share with Holly. Kisses are practically chaste in nature, but my cheeks heat ten degrees because there was nothing chaste about those kisses.

"*What*?" Holly squawks so loud Jenna bolts back in with a look of alarm.

"Never mind her." I shake my head at my clearly over-excitable sister. "Jenna? Can you man the counter? I'll finish loading the van. I think I just heard a customer come in."

"Sure thing." She takes off, and it's just Holly and me once again—with me glaring at my sister.

"It was nothing." I bite down over my bottom lip so hard I'm about to squirt blood.

"*Nothing*?" She laughs as she says it, her voice still hitting its upper register. Holly has always had the ability to see right through me—something I continually find annoying on every level. There are some things I'd like to keep to myself—case in point, Graham.

"Okay, it was everything, but don't you dare say I told you so." It *was* everything. It felt like the weight of the world lifted off my shoulders to admit it. Kissing Graham was like finally being able to exhale after a lifetime of holding my breath.

"Why wouldn't I say I told you so? Clearly I was right." She wraps another tray before sliding the entire project to her left. "Now, tell me every dirty little detail."

"There are no dirty details. The first time we kissed was at the tree lot. Sort of," I mumble out that last part. Technically, I kissed him—on the cheek. But in all fairness, it led to that very reciprocated kiss we shared in my living room after putting up my tree. That kiss outshined the star we eventually set on the highest bough.

"Aw!" she moans as if Noel just scampered into the room. That's pretty much the requisite reaction whenever anyone meets my pretty little pooch. She's so stinking adorable, I keep a picture of her in the office so I won't miss her that badly when I'm stuck at work. But oddly enough, I only seem to miss her more when I see it. "Did Nick hold up the mistletoe above your heads and take a picture? I'm betting he loved seeing his best friend hook up with his little sister."

"Oh, stop." Speaking of stopping, my heart gives an abnormal thud at the thought of my brother witnessing the event. "He doesn't know, and we're not going to tell him. We like our brother among the living, remember? Honestly, I think it'd kill him." I know it would. Nick has always been ultra protective of Holly and me. I'm still not quite sure how Tom got away with marrying my sister. I thought for sure Nick was going to take him out long before the nuptials. Nick just wants the best for us, and according to Nick, the "best" doesn't quite exist in nature.

She makes a face. "I'm thinking the only funeral to plan would be Graham's. Nick will want to stay around long enough to commit a proper homicide. So, when are the two of you going to make your debut as a couple? Whenever it is, make sure I'm there." A mischievous giggle bubbles from her.

"I seriously doubt we will." I lean my elbows onto the counter and take in a lungful of flour and sugar. "It doesn't seem possible for Graham and me to work. Nick and his homicidal intentions aside, Graham has carved out quite a spectacular life for himself in Manhattan. And I have this place." I cast a quick glance around at the mint green walls, and it feels so homey I'd swear the bakery just gave me a nice, warm hug.

"I'll take care of this place. You go to New York and shop on Fifth Avenue for me. That way I can come out every few weeks to inspect your purchases and see how you're doing." She gives a sly wink.

"Trust me, Graham and I are nowhere near shacking up together. And, believe me, that's not something I would do. New York is a million miles away. I couldn't just move there."

"Not even for love? For *true* love?"

Just as I'm about to pipe up once again, Mom breezes in, decked out in a black leather jacket and a pair of matching boots that hug those jeans of hers straight to her knees. My mother has always been a self-proclaimed fashionista, but the cool biker chick outfit she's sporting this afternoon has me feeling a serious bout of jacket envy.

"Who's in love?" Her arms flail every which way as if she were startled. "What'd I miss? When'd it happen?" She shoves a sugar cookie into her mouth and gives it a nervous nibble.

My mouth falls open once again to refute the claim. I might be in love with Graham Holiday, but there's no way I'm alerting the presses—and telling my mother would amount to the very same thing. But before I can utter a single word, a redheaded, equally clad in leather, Sabrina Jarrett struts right in with a look of homicidal intent that could rival that of my brother's should he get wind of that kiss that took place right under his proverbial nose.

"I'm the one in love." Sabrina manufactures a short-lived smile for my mother before looking sternly my way. "May I have a word with you, Mistletoe Winters? *Alone*."

Holly mobilizes as if we just received a tornado warning and scuttles Mom out to the café before I can protest. Alone is something I never want to be with Sabrina. It's no wonder Graham isn't interested. She's terrifying to be around once she has you in a room without another living being in sight.

Sabrina steps in close, her eyes slit to nothing. That gardenia perfume of hers is so overpowering my skin threatens to break out into hives, and I can already feel my throat locking off. It's a bit ironic that I'm not allergic to a single thing, but in all the years I've known Sabrina, she's elicited this very reaction in me whenever we're in close proximity. A part of me still wishes New York were a prospect as far as housing for the viper in front of me goes. But I could never do that to Graham. Not now anyway.

"Ida Bergman works at Peabody's Bookstore," she spits out every word as if it were venom.

Bookstore? *Bookstore*! My eyes round out for a moment, but I force them to return to their natural size as to not incite suspicion. My breathing grows erratic, and like a trained Navy SEAL, I command my body to take soothing, even breaths. Sabrina Jarrett is a master at smelling fear in people.

"Oh, really?" I give a few innocent blinks, praying that any skills I might have in the drama department quickly come to the forefront. "Do they need a platter of cookies? Brownies maybe for the employees?" I steal the moment to take a few trotting steps to the other side of the counter. I figure there's safety in a few hundred pounds of marble between us. "Just about every business on Main Street is having a holiday party this week. You'll have to excuse me. I need to get these cookies in the van and drive them over to the Boys and Girls Club."

Sabrina takes a few stalking steps in my direction. Her jaws set on a scowl, her eyes burning their venom right through me. "Sources say they spotted the two of you leaping around Peabody's, then skipping up and down Main Street holding hands like a couple of teenagers. Is that true?" That last sentence comes out as more of a roar, and I flinch as if she struck me.

"No, not at all!" Darn her book club posse for monitoring the mean streets of Gingerbread. "I simply went into Peabody's to pick up my yearly donation for the children's ward at the hospital. Graham happened to be there, and he helped me carry out several bags of books. There was no way we could have been holding hands. Our arms were full of enough parchment to furnish an entire Alaskan wilderness." A thought comes to me. "You know all about that toy drive. Your dad plays Santa for the event every year and distributes the gifts himself. And doesn't your mother read the children on the unit the Christmas story?" I coo as if I just saw Noel's sweet face for the very first time.

Her lips pull into a line. "I don't care about any of that. I care about Graham and me—as in the super couple you promised me we'd be. Didn't you win some ridiculous trophy for being the world's most prolific matchmaker? My relationship is falling apart at the seams. Do something!"

I swallow hard for two reasons. One, Sabrina Jarrett is yelling at me in a threatening tone. And two, I think I may have just forfeited my title as world's best matchmaker.

"Actually"—I hold up a finger, backing up as she slowly edges her way toward me—"I never said I was prolific. And if they were handing out trophies for such a thing, I'm pretty sure all I would come away with is a participation trophy. You know, the kind you get for just showing up?" Right about now, I'm wishing I had a very tangible trophy that I might use to knock her over the head while I make a run for it.

Sabrina bares her fangs at me, growling the way Noel does when I try to hide her teddy bear. "Listen up, *Missy*"— she makes my name sound like a putdown—"I'm this close to tripling your rent myself if you make one wayward move toward my boyfriend."

Her boyfriend? Wow, it looks like I really did a bang-up job on one end of the equation—the psychotic end that goes by the name of Sabrina Jarrett. She's obviously in love enough for the both of them. Just perfect. I've inadvertently gifted poor Graham a lifelong psychotic of his very own for Christmas. "Come up with some way to get that boy to have a conversation with me. Each time I call he won't pick up. I've sent a thousand text messages, too! And yesterday when I was coming out of the tree lot, I spotted him and he took off in the other *direction*! Sure, he was chasing that demented overgrown rat the two of you are warring over—and you will so win once I get him back. I assure you of that." She gives a feverish nod as if to sweeten the pot. "But as for now, our relationship is at a standstill." Her chest bucks, and I'm half - convinced the leather seams on that skintight jacket are about to burst. "You have to find a way to make this work again."

"Okay!" I pick up a spatula as if it were a weapon, and it may have to be. "I know what I need to do, and it just might get the train back on track. But you have to listen to me very carefully."

Her mouth gapes as she nods frenetically. "Yes, anything."

"Good." I tick my head to the side, shocked at how easy that was. "I will speak with Graham. It's vital for me to do so if I'm to ascertain exactly what might be going awry. Don't worry. I'll be covert. Sometimes men are simply aloof and have no idea that they're doing something wrong." I wince because pretty much everything I've just spewed from my lips is a bald-faced lie. "And then I need you to drive out to Holiday Orchards and find his brother." His brother? I have no clue where my mouth is about to take this, but I'm praying it's someplace where I get to keep my teeth. I wouldn't put it past Sabrina to employ those stilettos against me.

"His brother?" she spits the words out like she might be sick.

"Yeah, you know. Divide and conquer." I'm pretty sure that's not how divide and conquer works, but, let's face it, Sabrina isn't even getting a participation trophy as far as IQ scores go. "I'll talk to Graham and see what I find out, and you talk to his brother. There's not a person on this planet who knows Graham better. They grew up together. He's practically an insider." Okay, so I've just added another bald-faced lie to the collection. So sue me. And I'm starting to believe when this entire fiasco blows up in my face, Sabrina might just go and do that.

"Just know this"—my voice hikes a notch as if I were dishing out a threat of my own—"my investigation might take some time—so don't be surprised if my assessment takes a little longer than anticipated."

"Like how long?"

I give an uncertain shrug. "A *week*?" That will buy me all the time I need with Graham right up until he boards his private jet back to Manhattan. Oh my goodness! Does Graham have a private jet? Honestly, that just might be a game changer. Maybe I should knock some sense into Sabrina with this spatula after all. There's no real reason to continue on with this farce—with the exception of the bakery. I openly scowl at the marble island. If it wasn't for Holly, I might actually play Jarrett roulette with it. *Triple my rent.* I'm going to kiss Graham twice as much today just to spite her.

"A week?" She shakes her head as if it were a deal breaker.

"If you want to speed things along, then I suggest you spend all the time you can with Tanner. And if you can't find him at the orchard, he's probably in Cater. If I were you, I'd practically shackle myself to the man. And—for the sake of your love life and my reputation as the world's most prolific matchmaker, I'll do the same with Graham."

She comes in close, her eyes widening like twin hard-boiled eggs as if she sees right through my little boyfriend-snatching scheme. Not that he was ever hers for me to snatch. Nope. It turns out, Graham has been mine all along. At least that's what my matchmaker instincts tell me.

"Perfect!" she bleats so loud it sounds as if a bomb just detonated in the kitchen.

"Perfect?" I squeak with disbelief.

"It's genius actually. The more time we spend with the Holiday boys, the quicker I'll get my clutches on the right Holiday altogether." She scrambles toward the café. "I'm headed out to find Tanner asap. And if you're smart, you'll be with Graham within the next ten minutes." She turns, and that narrow-eyed glare of hers is right back on me. "You have until Christmas Eve to repair what's broken. Or you can kiss your little bakery goodbye." She takes off, and I place the spatula over my heart and let out a sigh of relief.

My phone buzzes in my pocket, and I fish it out. It's a text from Graham.

You up for a quick walk around the lake? Noel says she likes it better when you hold the leash.

I can't help but laugh when I read it. I text right back. **Meet me at the Boys and Girls Club in fifteen minutes. It's a date.**

What Sabrina doesn't know won't kill her. But as soon as she finds out, she just might kill me—and my little bakery, too.

I don't dare give Holly the proper rundown on what happened between Sabrina and me. There's no way I'll ruin her Christmas by letting her in on the fact her livelihood is in peril. Sure, Tom makes great money as an optometrist, but face it—Gingerbread isn't all that big, and he's fixed just about every eyeball within our city limits. If they want to add to their brood, and put Savanah and Baby X through college, they'll need a thriving second income. And when she finds out that my little matchmaking scheme has backfired on me spectacularly, I might just let her say I told you so—just this once. It's the least I could do after she realizes she'll be losing her home. I'll lose my home, too, and we'll both end up back with our parents in our old bedrooms. Only she'll be sharing a twin with Tom and Savanah, and I'll be in mine with Noel. In theory, my scenario seems far rosier, but in truth, Noel kicks like a mule in her sleep. I'm liable to end up with a broken nose and six cracked ribs. I'm pretty sure Sabrina will find some creative, yet equally destructive, way to make Graham's life miserable, too. Like flying to New York on her broomstick and tossing a Molotov cocktail through his penthouse window. My God, she's going to reduce his entire building to cinders, altering the lives of thousands of people, all because I had the urge to teach Graham Holiday a lesson.

I guess the only one learning a lesson around here is me.

My little foray into revenge just might cost me everything.

I try my best to shake Sabrina and her volatile threats out of my mind as I get back to loading the van, but the effort proves impossible. I tell both Jenna and Holly that I'll do the run myself. As much as I'm looking forward to spending time with Graham this afternoon, I'm deathly afraid of what will happen once Sabrina discovers my little ruse.

By the time I finish getting the very last platter of sugar cookies into the Boys and Girls Club, I find both Graham and Noel seated on the rear bumper of the van when I get back.

"Hey, hot stuff." An ear-to-ear grin springs to my face as I say it. "Can I get a picture with you?"

Graham's lids hang low as if he were suddenly trying to seduce me, and, dear God, it takes far less than that to do it. "Would you like it with my clothes on or off?"

"*Gah!*" I swat him with my purse as if he were a mugger. "I was talking to Noel. But since you're here, I don't see why the three of us don't take a few selfies by the lake. I hear you can see clear across to Cater. And if I remember correctly, if we stand on the highest peak of the bridge, you can see the smokestack from a certain pie factory that's about to explode onto the culinary scene as the latest greatest sensation. I wouldn't be surprised if the Food Channel wanted to do an exposé on you."

Graham belts out a laugh as he stands and caresses my cheek with his thumb. "I was thinking about doing a few exposés myself. On you. So much has changed. You're all grown up, and I want to know everything there is about you. You know, fill in the blanks—tell me what I missed."

I bite down on my lip while looking up at this god who has generously chosen to grace my world. "I think we'd better hurry and get to the lake. It sounds like we have a lot of ground to cover."

151

I jump into his truck as we drive to the outskirts of town where an expansive body of water shimmers a fantastic shade of crystalline blue—the exact color of Graham Holiday's eyes.

"It's so beautiful," I whisper as we get out and marvel as the snow meets the water. "There is nothing more breathtaking than seeing the sky kiss the water. And when you add snow to the equation, the world just becomes that much more enchanting."

Graham wraps his arms around my waist from behind and lands a careful kiss just under my ear. "I can think of at least one thing—one *person* far more breathtaking than any of the above."

I spin in his arms and can't help but bite down a smile. "Noel?"

He inches back playfully perturbed. "How'd you guess?"

She nips and barks as if trying to get our attention while tugging wildly at the leash. "Speaking of which"—I take a few steps out with her, and she's pulling hard to get right into a giant field full of fluffy white powder—"I think she's a little snow fiend."

"Yeah, well, I suppose there are far more nefarious things to covet. Why don't we head over and make all of her frozen dreams come true?"

Graham and I wade in ankles deep as Noel all but does a somersault with glee.

He yanks a pair of gloves out of his jacket and hands them to me. "I've got a great idea," he says before producing yet another pair and donning them himself.

"Have gloves will travel." I pull them on, and my fingers instantly warm back to life. "Thank you. This was very thoughtful of you."

His left eye comes shy of winking. "Never leave the house without them. You never know when the mood to build a snowman will strike."

"Snowman!" I pick up a pile of the white stuff and toss it over our heads, causing frozen chunks of ice to pelt us. "It's on," I say, bending over and greedily gathering all the snow around me as if it were a scarce commodity. "I'll make mine ten times bigger than yours, Holiday!"

"I wasn't thinking about a competition." He falls next to me and starts assisting me in the effort. "I was sort of hoping we could work on one together." His blue eyes latch to mine, and their bold color gives both the lake and the sky a run for their cobalt money. "I was sort of hoping we could do a lot of things together. You know, like a real couple."

A breath catches in my throat. "A couple?" My mouth falls open. "Why, Graham Holiday—did you just ask me to be your girlfriend?" I invoke my infamous country accent that I used to drive him insane with way back when. He loved it then, but he would never admit it.

"Why yes, I did, Sprig. So, what do you say?" His features grow serious, and the air around us stills as if it, too, were anticipating my response. "You in?"

"I'm in." I lean forward as if I'm about to plant a good one on him, and deep down I know that if I start, I will never want to stop. "I can build this snowman singlehandedly in less than five minutes!" I shriek, and he laughs right along with me as we slap together the world's roundest, perhaps most unstable snowman on the planet. I find a pair of black stones for its eyes, and Graham finds a stubby little stick for the nose and branches for its arms. The two of us stand back a moment and admire our work of art, panting and red-faced from the effort.

Graham slings his arm around my shoulders. "How about we take that picture now of the three of us? We can use it as our Christmas card."

A quiet laugh brews in me as I scratch at his chest, my head resting on his shoulder. "That sounds great, but it might not get out until next year. I'm pretty swamped this week."

Graham glances down, his lips upturned at the idea. "Next year? I like the sound of that."

"Me, too."

We call Noel over, and Graham picks her up while I struggle to get the three of us and our lopsided snowman all in the same frame. Eventually I do, and I take picture after picture to prove it.

"You ready for that walk around the lake?" He lands a heated kiss to the top of my head, and that simple action makes me feel as if I were the most special girl in all the world.

I shake my head as I look up at him from under my lashes. "My lips are a little cold. I was hoping maybe you could warm them."

His dimples ignite as he washes over me with those daring blue eyes. "I've got an idea, but it will take time."

"The best things always do."

Graham lands his mouth over mine, softly, deliberately—right here in the open, and it feels as if we've just crested into brand new territory. His arms fold around me as he holds me tight, and our kisses pick up pace as if the fate of the planet depended on this one perfect moment. Graham and I ignite a blaze right here in the snow, heating up the vicinity with the fire of a thousand suns.

Deep down, I always knew that kissing Graham Holiday would be hotter than a kitchen fire. I just never figured that I would be lucky enough to be on the receiving end of that inferno. And boy am I ever glad all of the vengeful stars aligned this fateful December and landed this beautiful man in my arms, his mouth fused over mine. Graham and his singeing kisses are all I ever want for the rest of my life.

What I feel for Graham burns brighter than any flame.

If this is what it feels like to fall in love, then all I can say is *burn, baby, burn.*

Graham

Icicles line the branches of the evergreen boughs, the shadows from the forest cast a blue hue over the sparkling snow, and every rooftop visible to the human eye is laden with a thick coat of sugary icing that fell from the sky. There is nothing more intoxicating than Gingerbread in winter—with the exception of Mistletoe Winters. Yes, Missy is the finest wine, and those kisses have made me drunk off our love. I had seen people I know fall hard and fast—watched their affect change, their habits, and ultimately their legal status, as one by one my friends have gotten married. I swore it wouldn't happen to me. It seemed unnatural, as if they were suddenly under a spell and they had no control over their good senses. It never seemed to happen slowly. It was always so quick. One moment they were hanging out in bars with you, and the next they couldn't pencil you in for coffee. They had a place to be, and it wasn't with their friends. It was that invisible leash I swore I would never don, and here I don't want to move an inch away from Missy, let alone spend hours a day apart. I get it. It happened fast, and it happened hard. I'm in love with Missy.

A goofy grin glides over my face as I drive through the countryside on my way to the family orchard. I've been back in Gingerbread for three weeks now, and I'm just now getting

ADDISON MOORE

around to making the trek. And as much as I feel bad about it, I refuse to let the guilt get to me. Over the last few years, Tanner has never made me feel welcome on that plot of earth that's been in my family for generations. It shouldn't come as a surprise to him that it's the last place I want to be.

Noel barks up a storm as we near the orchard as if she could feel the excitement of the ranch herself. It'll be her first time on the property, and I know she'll love it. It's acre after acre of free roaming and enough backwoods to get lost in for a year. I plan on keeping her leashed for the most part, but once she looks at me with those sad brown eyes, I know I'll have to let her loose. She's been pretty good about bouncing right back to me after her playful forays into the unknown. I guess she understands what side her bread is buttered on—and thanks to Missy, it's buttered with only the finest ingredients. I'm pretty sure Noel is on the crème de la crème of doggie diets—and for Noel, I wouldn't want it any other way.

Tanner sent a cryptic text this morning, so I thought instead of texting back, I'd head up to the orchard to hear what he has to say myself. Besides, what's better than the element of surprise to see what's really going on at this place day to day?

I drive under the large iron sign that reads *Welcome to Holiday Orchards!* and a chill runs through me. Even when I was a kid, driving under that monolithic banner gave me a sense of pride. It made me feel as though my family was truly special and that anything we set out to do in this world was for our taking. Success runs in my family, and I've clung to that fact for years. It's what's fueled me along the way in becoming one of New York's most prominent selling realtors. I simply believed that I could do it, that success was an inevitable part of the equation—and it seems to be. Sometimes in life that's all you need, a little faith to bolster you to where you need to be. It can take you to the stratosphere every single time.

I park out by the sturdy oak, with its sprawling wingspan, just shy of the barn. Noel races from window to window as I glance down at the text one more time before getting out of the truck. **Just a heads-up, you're under investigation.**

I have no clue what my brother is babbling about. Noel and I jump out and take in a lungful of fresh Holiday Orchard air, and she tugs and bites at the leash, already wanting a taste of freedom. It's crisp out, the sky is a comfortable shade of gray, and I take a moment to feast my eyes on the grounds where the foundation of my life was laid.

The orchards to the far right have netting around them and sheeting to protect the more fragile trees from the frost. The garden just beyond that is buried in snow at the moment. There's a greenhouse the size of a shopping mall in the distance, and it glows a beautiful shade of emerald. That's where the seeds germinate for spring plantings, and anything that can't survive the winter gets stored in. To my left, the barn sits tall and proud. The paint is chipping and the color has faded to a rosy pink, but it welcomes me with its toothless smile like that of an old faithful friend. The main house sits just behind it with cheery peach lights on in various rooms.

Mom and Dad called this morning and let me know they were headed to Denver to take care of a few last-minute holiday details, but the house is most likely being prepped for their annual Christmas dinner by a small crew my mother hires for the event. Every year they invite a few dozen friends to share in the feast. It's become a time-honored tradition that those who make the cut look forward to. I used to look forward to the event myself, still do.

Behind the main house there are at least six cottages that dot the property. Tanner has made the biggest one his home. I have no clue what kind of luck he's had with the ladies, but I'd hate to think he's spending one too many lonely nights in that thing. As much as Tanner and I have distanced ourselves from one another, I really do care about my brother. And being alone is no way to live.

A familiar looking dude with a dove gray cowboy hat planted over his head strides out of the barn with a wheelbarrow treading in front of him, and I jog on over.

"Tanner Holiday." I flash a quick grin his way before looking into the manure pile he's laden his cart with. "Still slinging bull, I see. Some things never change."

He takes off his hat and wipes the sweat from his brow. "I keep forgetting to laugh whenever you're around. I see you brought your better half." He bends over, and Noel makes a beeline for him, licking his face and giving him all the love she has to offer. Noel is clearly a lover and not a fighter. And it's becoming quickly apparent she's not choosing sides between my brother and me.

"She definitely brings out the best in people." Noel keeps trying to get deeper into the barn so I drop the leash and let her run wild as she darts inside. "So, what's up? You sic the IRS on me? Or did you find someone far more lethal to teach me a lesson?"

He grunts as he leads us to the wet bar inside the barn. Yes, there is a bona fide granite counter with stools dotting around the outskirts with enough seating for ten people. My mother thought that the ranch hands needed to take a seat and have a nice cold drink once in a while. The full-sized fridge next to it is stocked with tea and lemonade mostly, and there's a microwave for reheating food if needed. She also had a few bathrooms installed in the back, taking our barn to the next employee lunchroom level.

Tanner pulls out a bottle of water for the both of us before plopping down next to me.

He falls forward on his elbows, hanging his head a moment as if claiming defeat. "Why'd you do it? Why'd you train her on me?"

"Train who? Are *you* being investigated by the IRS?" My heart thumps wildly because I wouldn't do that to anybody. I learned a long time ago that messing with the IRS was like catching a tiger by the tail. No thanks. I like my body parts just where they are.

"Sabrina Jarrett." His dark brows dip down, and he looks decidedly like me after a rough morning in the gym, far too red-faced and sweaty for my own good.

I lean back in my seat and marvel for a moment. "So that's where she went." It's been a blissful week of almost zero contact from the woman, save for the daily texts wishing me a good day, letting me know she's thinking about me, sending me snapshots of her feet propped up while in the bathtub. Thankfully, that's as explicit as those pictorials have gotten. But there's a thin rail of terror in me whenever I get another message from her. You never know when Sabrina will be moved to take things to the next level.

He inches his head back. "What do you mean 'that's where she went'? She's been here all week hounding me for information about you. Now she's hanging around, pretending to be interested in every facet of the orchard. She even hitched a ride to the factory with me yesterday. We were there for six hours, and she followed along as though she were on some sort of an internship. Did you put her up to this? And for God's sake, why?"

My mouth opens for a moment. I can't seem to figure this out. "I didn't put her up to anything. She's been after me ever since I set foot in town. She kept alluding to the fact we're meant to be." My jaw grinds hard. "Meant to be a safe distance from one another is more like it." I down a third of my water bottle before turning to my brother.

"*Huh.*" He studies me a moment. "You do seem rather clueless."

"What's that supposed to mean?"

"It means what it always means. You come into town, shocked to hear the factory is closing, and yet you haven't even looked at the finances in years. How did it feel getting out of that fancy truck of yours today? I bet the landscape looked foreign. There's not a thing on this ranch you've seen or touched in a decade. It's all on me. Every frigging tree that's standing is standing because of my care, my hands. After Dad retired, he left everything to *us*. What a joke. The only thing you're good at is collecting a fat paycheck at the end of the month."

"It's not that fat." I can't help but stick him with the dig. I don't like his tone or the fact he's inferring that I don't care. I do care. Something deep inside of me cinches because I'm not quite sure how true that rings.

"Those checks might be a little fatter if you gave a damn." He knocks back his water. "A lot of things might be different around here if I had a hand or two helping me out where I really need it—marketing, sales. I'm too busy doing the grunt work to put my head where it really belongs. Instead of working smarter, I'm working harder." He gets up and makes his way back to his wheelbarrow. "You know what that feels like? It feels like I've got a giant boulder the size of New York City planted over my chest, and I can't get out from under it." He glares at me a moment. "Go on. Get out of here. I bet you can't wait to get back to New York just to make that boulder on my chest that much heavier. It's what you do best." He takes off, and my body goes numb from the sting of his words. As much as I want to speed the heck away from this place, from my brother and his glaring accusations, I can't seem to move. A part of me knows he was speaking the truth. And in this instance, the truth very much feels like a knife to the chest.

I muster the strength to collect Noel, and we hop into the truck and drive through the back roads of the orchard while I let that entire conversation sink down to the marrow in my bones.

I hate that I've become a weight for my brother.

I have never wanted to hurt him.

And I have.

Downtown Gingerbread is lit up from top to bottom with its zigzagging twinkle lights strung high over Main Street. Every roofline, pole, and wreath is wrapped with its own string of lights, and the enchanting visual alone makes me realize I've missed Gingerbread far too much to ever be away for long spates of time. New York City definitely has a charm of its own, but it's not home. I don't think it ever can be.

And on this magical night, I've asked Missy to dinner at what looks to be Gingerbread's newest fine dining facility. But it's not the delicious meal I'm looking forward to most. It's the stunning woman by my side.

Missy and I find a parking spot right in front of Le Roux, and I hop out to help her out of the passenger's side. Missy Winters outshines every last light bulb in this tiny town combined, not to mention the fact she puts the stars and all their glory to shame.

"Sprig"—I say as I pull her in close, our eyes locking with a boost of electricity that lets me know I'm in far too deep to ever get out—"you take my breath away. You look beautiful tonight."

She wrinkles her nose at me, looking decidedly adorable in the process. "Thank you—for the fifteenth time." Her strawberry stained lips twist to the side. "You know, you don't have to keep repeating it, but if it makes you feel better, I'll be the last person to stop you." The apples of her cheeks fill with color. "I'm rather partial to hearing it from the horse's mouth." Her thumb swipes over my lips. "And I do love this horse's mouth." Her brows dip with concern. "Do you think Noel will be fine with Holly and Tom?"

"Are you kidding? After seeing Savanah's face light up like the sun, we'll be lucky to get her back tonight."

"That's true. And technically, this is Savy's first babysitting job. I know she's pretty excited about the puppy. Maybe more so than the fact she's getting paid." She shivers as she pulls her black wool coat tight around her tiny body.

"Let's get you inside before we turn into Popsicles."

"I thought you liked Popsicles?" Her eyes flirt with mine as she bats her lashes. "You know, licking them up until the very last drop."

"Whoa!" I tug at the collar of my dress shirt. "And it's suddenly way too hot to have this coat on." I tuck my hand on the small of her back, and we head inside where the subtle scent of something homey cooking thickens the air.

I've never been to Le Roux before. It's a new addition to Gingerbread since the days in which I regularly roved these streets. It's dark inside, dim to be exact, and it feels as if candles power the entire restaurant. The maître d' leads us to a private table near a window in the front, and Missy looks down at it with apprehension. I know she's not hot on her family—namely her brother—discovering anything about us before we've had a chance to explain things formally to everyone. And the reason that hasn't happened yet is because we're still trying to figure things out ourselves. This would have been much easier if we had met in New York. No past, no thorny family history to have laid out before us like an obstacle course.

I pull out her seat and help her off with her coat, revealing a bright blue dress that clings to her in all the right places. My God, Missy Winters has really shaped up nicely in the most literal sense, and I feel like a dog for scouring her with my gaze.

"My eyes are up here, sweetheart." She flicks a finger over my cheek playfully as I take a seat across from her.

"And what gorgeous eyes you have." I lean in a moment and just lose myself in their hypnotic powers. "Has science classified a unique phylum for your family yet? I'm pretty sure those eyes are anything but human."

Her pink glossy lips round out into a perfect O. "Are you calling the entire Winters family subhuman?" Her eyes sparkle and dance, and for the life of me, I don't ever want this perfect moment to end.

"I'm calling you out of this world."

"Oh, now that's an improvement!" She belts out a laugh just as a couple strides by, but Missy and I don't dare take our eyes off one another. The couple stops cold, and I glance up, only to do a double take.

"What the heck?" Nick Winters looks as if he just caught us chopping the tails off a litter of puppies.

"*Mom!*" Missy's alien eyes nearly fall out of their sockets.

"Missy?" Mrs. Winters looks to me with horror before her mouth rounds out with surprise. "Graham Holiday!" she squeals and stomps her foot to the floor three times fast. She sucks in another lungful of air and clutches at her chest. "Oh my goodness, this is a date, isn't it!"

Nick folds his arms over his chest and silently slaughters me with that merciless stare.

"No way," Missy protests loud and clear, and my gut cinches because a part of me wishes we could have come clean. It's just days before Christmas. It would have been perfect to let them in on our burgeoning secret.

"Hey, dude." Nick kicks me in the shoe and ticks his head for me to follow him. "Excuse us," he says to his mother before shooting Missy a dark look. "I need to get Graham's opinion on something to do with the lot."

Missy glances my way with a disbelieving scowl. Neither of us is buying this tree lot baloney. Looks like I don't have the only brother who likes to sling some bull.

Nick stalks over to the corner of the foyer before spinning into me with venom ready to spit out of him. "Are you seeing my sister?"

"What? Me and Sprig? What's gotten into you, man?" My heart thumps a mile a minute, and as much as I'd want to say something to set him straight, I can tell he's too amped up to handle any news I might be willing to give him. Right now, I just want to take off without him gifting me a black eye. There's no way I want to break it to Nick like this, in some hallway separated by Missy by what feels like miles. Nope. We should both be present when we break it to Nick. "Look, she's a nice kid, but we're just a couple of old friends trying to enjoy dinner out." There. That should allow him to rest easy for tonight. And when Missy and I are ready to tell him about us, he can gift me the black eye then. Although a sick feeling has suddenly come to rest in the pit of my stomach. I couldn't look Nick in the eye when I spewed those half-truths.

"At a French restaurant?" He nods with his eyes bulging the way Missy's were a minute ago. "What kind of dude brings a friend to a place like this?"

"The same kind that brings his mother." I had to go there. He practically shoved me into it. "Look, we're hungry. Missy is exhausted, and I was on my way out. She mentioned that your niece wanted a night with Noel, and I asked if she wanted to grab a bite." Not the entire truth, but somewhere in there the details are all structurally correct. "Trust me, not in a million years could I see myself ending up with your sister." Not up until a few weeks ago when it all became clear as that lake that sits on the edge of town. I do my best to keep that goofy grin from buoying back to my lips. I can't help it. I can truly see myself ending up with his sister, and the thought makes me want to smile like a loon all day long.

His chin remains tucked to his chest. "And you just so happened to score a window seat at the busiest restaurant in town on a Friday night?" He closes his eyes a moment, his chest rumbling. "Maybe Tanner is right. You are the golden boy, and a window seat at Le Roux is just something that happens for you." His brows harden as he makes it no secret to let me know how ticked he is. "It took my mother a week to get this reservation. My father couldn't make it. I'm his stand-in." He leans in and jabs a finger into my chest like a bullet. "Stay away from my sister or this will be your last meal." He shoves his way out the door, and an iced breeze snakes in past him.

"Night, night!" Joy Winters blows me an air kiss as she sprints out the door to catch up with her overprotective son.

I head back to the table and gird myself for whatever might come next. Perhaps an epic breakup before we get to any other would-be epic event.

"Are you still speaking to me?" I wince as I take a seat.

Her brows hike into her forehead. "According to my mother, we're getting hitched at the community center Sunday night for all of Gingerbread to witness." She sighs while cracking open her menu.

"A Christmas Eve wedding? Nick might let me attend, but he'll make sure I spend our wedding night at the morgue."

Her lips pull back as if she might be sick. "I guess my brother isn't onboard with the idea."

"He's not even onboard with the *hint* of an idea."

The waitress appears and takes our orders—we both agree to try the specials since neither of us is familiar with French food, and our dinner is delivered in record time.

Missy and I make small talk, laugh about the past, and circle around the future as if it didn't exist. But judging by that megawatt smile of hers, of mine, the laughter that never seems to cease between us, the future doesn't really matter, not tonight anyway. Missy and I are sure of one thing, each other.

Once we're through, we head back out into a festive Gingerbread night as the crowds gather down by the official town tree lit with ten thousand bright lights. Carolers stroll up and down Main Street decked out in traditional Dickens' garb, their voices melding together as they sing "Deck the Halls" with its cheerful refrain.

Missy reaches over and takes up my hand, our fingers threading together effortlessly, and it feels like a milestone, like maybe there is a future for us after all.

A horse-drawn carriage, forged to resemble a well-lit sleigh, jingles its way down the street, and Missy gives an enthusiastic hop when she sees it.

"It's Santa's sleigh! Oh, Holly and I used to come down every year and ride it up and down Main Street. It was so much fun. But she has Tom and Savanah now. It's been years since I've been on that thing."

"*Hey!*" I flag down the driver, and he comes to an abrupt stop. The ornate bobsled is lined with garland, and every last inch of it glows with twinkle lights.

"What are you doing?" she gasps as though she were truly frightened. "Are you crazy? We can't parade ourselves up and down Main Street. That's the least platonic thing in the world. Someone might see us! And worse yet, someone might misconstrue what's happening, thereby causing every business establishment on Main Street to experience a rent hike!"

The driver backs up, leaving me no time to decode what just streamed from Missy's beautiful lips.

"Can you go down Bloomwood instead?" I point to the street to our left, and the driver gives a thumbs-up. "We're in." I help a giggling Missy inside first before sliding next to her with my arm wrapped around her shoulders.

She looks up at me with her jaw to the floor as if the act of wrapping my arm around her were entirely salacious.

"What?" I can't help but grin at her. "Baby, it's cold outside." I pull her in tight as the horses trot off at a decent clip. The glowing sleigh we're in glides down the street and makes a sharp left onto far darker, far quieter territory.

Missy snuggles in close, her hand scratching over my chest as she bats those impossibly long lashes at me. "I can't believe we're doing this!" Her affect changes on a dime, and it looks as if she's about to cry. "I can't believe I'm doing this with *you*. You were my first real crush, Graham Holiday." Her smile melts quickly. "My first real heartbreak."

A hard groan comes from me. "What did I do now?" It doesn't matter. I'm already disappointed in myself for it.

"You didn't do anything." She reaches up and scratches the scruff on my cheeks. "You simply got on with life and moved to New York. I just chalked it up to destiny and the fact we both must have different ones."

My heart warms as much as it breaks to hear it. "Nope. I'm back, and it's safe to say destiny played a big part in that." Here Missy is, in my arms, looking like an angel that drifted down from heaven, and I want nothing more than to tell her she'll always have me in her life, but my stomach knots up because that leaves New York with a giant question mark over it. Instead, I muster up the strength to tell her the one thing I know for sure. "Have I told you how beautiful you look tonight?"

A throaty laugh escapes her as she gives me a playful swat. "Only about two dozen times. Is that your best one-liner?"

"I've got one more, but I've been saving it just for you." I swallow hard as my eyes steel over hers. "I love you, Missy. I have loved you for so long, and I didn't know what to do with it. There's no one else for me—just you." I give a slight nod as she tries to drink down what this might mean.

"Oh, Graham"—she wraps her arms around me tight and offers a firm embrace before pulling back, her lavender eyes hooking to mine—"I love you, too." Her lips press together tight. "I've always thought you were way out of my league, and I can't imagine why you'd even consider me as a prospect, but I'm glad you do." Her cheeks flood with color. "I have loved you for far longer than I even wanted to admit to myself."

I gently curl a finger under her chin. "You are in the only league I'm interested in—a league of your own. There's just you. I love you, Mistletoe Winters."

Her cheek glides up one side seductively, and carefully I land my lips to hers. Missy and I share a kiss that answers all the tough questions about the nebulous future. It's happening. It's ours. It's within our grasp.

We share passionate kisses, dark and deep, that explode the lid off any platonic theory I may have sold to her brother. And as much as I might be sorry for Nick, in no way am I sorry for us. Nope. Missy and I are happening. And no matter how ambiguous the future might be, we're going to figure it out together.

I'm in love with Mistletoe Winters.

And she's in love with me.

5

All is not Calm

Missy

When I was little, Christmas Eve meant waking up to the delicious scent of fritters frying over a hot stove. The thick scent would waft into my bedroom and wake me with the promise of doughy goodness. I would tread on sleepy feet over to the kitchen and indulge in one piping hot fritter after another, pungent with lemon zest, a slight hint of booziness from the vanilla, and plump golden raisins that my mother would throw into the batter. It was a little piece of fresh fried heaven in every single bite. It was my mother who gave me a love of baking, a love of freeing my spirit in the kitchen while taking my taste buds to sweet heavenly places. But this bustling Christmas Eve morning, I was awakened with neither the fresh scent of fritters nor the welcoming smile of my mother—instead, I was greeted with a seven-foot evergreen turned on its side, ornaments rolled out into the four corners of the living room. Noel ate her way through most of the wooden ornaments I dared decorate the tree with. And when I found her, she was tangled in Christmas lights, looking every bit adorable and guilty. To top it all off, she left a fresh batch of doggie brownies right in front of a gift I bought and wrapped for Graham. I'll admit that I laughed a little at that one, but only after I cried at the sight of the mess.

Once I sent her to *Daddy's*—and yes, I melt each time I refer to him that way—I showered and hightailed it to the bakery. And all of that was at four in the morning. Suffice it to say, this is turning out to be one long day.

It's now well past ten. Holly and I are losing our minds scrambling along with the rest of the team to put together a half a million cookie platters for the auction tonight. And even though I've been done for days, I can't stop putting the finishing touches on the gingerbread dollhouses taking up precious real estate in the back of the shop. I've long since sent Mayor Todd the gingerbread dollhouse for his girls, and I've walked over to the city hall on a few occasions to visit it. I must admit, it is a stunning sight to witness. The second one I've erected and decorated is the one I made for Savanah. I know she'll be thrilled when she wakes up tomorrow morning and sees it filled with the mountain of Barbies that

Mom and I purchased to go along with it. Holly accused me of spoiling her, but I let her know that as Savanah's only crazy aunt, it's basically my duty.

"Move faster!" Holly cries as she struggles to sprinkle a tray of freshly frosted sugar cookies with edible gold dust. Technically, all gold dust is edible, but the gold dust we're using amounts to metallic sugar in its yummiest form. Anytime that we place a batch of golden goodies into the showcase out front, they inevitably sell out. There's just something decadent about shoving a sweet gold nugget into your mouth. It makes you feel as if you're a part of the aristocracy, and tonight at the auction, it's all about making people feel as if they belong to a royal gentry. Even though Gingerbread is the most down-to-earth, cozy little town on this planet, once a year on the night of our dear Lord's birth, we like to kick up our heels while donning our finest frocks. Gilded cookies sort of feel like a given.

"I can't move faster," I whimper. "If I move any faster, everything I touch will end up on the floor. You know I'm a klutz in these situations." It's true. The faster I'm to move, the slower things get. God forbid that I find myself in a position where my life depended on the agility of my fingers while I'm forced to move under pressure. I'm sure any thief that targeted me would be more than sorry he chose the wrong victim—most likely I would be sorry, too.

Mom rushes in with her hair pulled back into a low ponytail and a red sequined Santa hat pressed over her head. "I've got half the van loaded, girls!" She tosses her arms in the air like a showgirl. My mother never lets a hectic situation get her frazzled. In fact, I believe she thrives on chaos—thus, the three children under five by the time she was thirty. "Let's wrap it up and move it out!"

Holly and I hustle the rest of the platters into the van at breakneck speeds before finally loading ourselves inside as well. In a mad panic, I drive the three of us straight to the community center, parking out back in the drop-off area that's already rife with people. The bustle of bodies moves in a frenetic pace as if each one of us felt as if we were falling behind schedule. It's the same every year, and each year the energy level of those working behind the scenes only seems to amplify itself. It's a beehive from sun up until well after the silent auction closes, and I don't think any of us would want it any other way. The Christmas Eve auction is the biggest yearly event in Gingerbread, and we work hard to keep all of the magic that comes with it alive.

"Coming through!" I call out as the three of us make trip after trip into the extra-large kitchen attached to the center. A tall woman dressed as an elf has set aside an entire row of tables just for the desserts, and we laden it with yummy treats from the bakery. As much as I love this time of year, I am always thrilled once the benefit begins because it's the first time in a month that I can truly relax. Part of the fun of the evening is getting dressed up in a nice dress and heels—*heels*. My feet don't even know how to behave in those manmade stilts, let alone dance in them. But there will be a band here tonight and lots and lots of dancing, so the heels inevitably come off right after dinner. It's always fun to see the postman cutting loose with the women from Curl Up and Dye. And who doesn't love watching the girls from Sabrina's snobby book club get ripped while downing one too many cups of eggnog?

Sabrina. Just the mention of her steals all the Christmas spirit right out of my heart.

Mom and Holly are schlepping in the last of the platters as I head into the main dining hall to sneak a peek at the elegant holiday décor that's fit for the finest of establishments. Thick ropes of garland skip around the room, just under the ceiling, giving the place an ironic gingerbread appeal. Lights are woven throughout the boughs, and come evening we'll feel as if we were transported to the inside of a castle that belongs in a fairy tale. But the pièce de résistance is that twenty-foot blue noble decked out in red ribbons and bows, enough sparkling ornaments to fill a warehouse with, and each branch is twined neatly with enough lights to ensure you can see the spectacle clear up to the space station. Yes, Gingerbread might be small, but we are mighty when it comes to displaying the love of our favorite holiday.

A tall, all too familiar, redhead strides into the room along with a group of scowling men—all who seem to be begrudgingly following her.

"I'll need these long tables moved to the front. I want to look out and see the people!" she orders, and the men mobilize as if she were about to hold their feet to the flames, and I have no doubt she is. "And I'll need the podium and the microphone set behind me. I'd like for these two seats to be in the direct path of the spotlight while Mayor Todd gives his welcome speech."

I can't help but make a face. I have a sneaking suspicion I know who she plans on seating in those soon-to-be brightly lit places. My feet start in on an awkward dance as I struggle to tiptoe out of the room unnoticed.

A pair of hands comes up from behind, tickling my sides, and I let out a shrill yelp. I turn to find Holly laughing her head off, but I'm guessing she won't be for long.

"Mistletoe Winters!" Sabrina grates my name out like the sound of nails on a long, never-ending chalkboard. In fact, I've never hated the sound of my name more than when it comes straight out of her mouth. No wonder Graham couldn't stand to be near her. He probably has nightmares that consist solely of her screeching his name out.

Holly gives me a slight push in that direction. "Be brave," she hisses as she scuttles back to the kitchen like a coward.

"Sabrina!" My feet glide forward like the traitors they are. "What can I do for you?" Other than secure your mouth with duct tape. A stale smile floats to my lips.

Her garish red lips look glossed with gear oil, and that formfitting, red velvet outfit makes me want to find the nearest robe and wrap her in it. Her vacuum-sealed curves don't exactly leave a lot to the imagination, not that Sabrina ever does. And FYI, I already know what she wants—my man. Something warms in me at the thought of Graham Holiday belonging exclusively to me. And he does.

Her lips expand to dangerous parameters. Her dark coal eyes each look like their own dark cave—caves that not even the bravest of souls would ever want to venture in.

"You know what you can do for me." She folds her hands together a moment, each fingernail alternating in color from red to green. "I expect to find Graham Holiday seated next to me for dinner, right over there." She points to where the podium is being placed just behind the seats of honor. "Great news." She leans in, a giddy wave of excitement shivers through her. "We're switching things up this year. Mayor Todd will be crowning a lucky couple as king and queen of the dance."

"A what?" I shake my head, trying desperately to keep up with her level of crazy. I'll have you know, it's not easy.

"Think prom, silly. It's been so long since I've had any kind of a title attached to my name, I just thought it was time, you know?"

"No, I don't know. This is the auction that benefits the community center. It's also Christmas Eve. I think that's enough excitement for one night, don't you agree?" A prom? A *prom*? She can't be serious. I knew that Sabrina Jarrett could find any excuse to don a tiara, but this is ridiculous. And pulling the entire town into her madness seems a bit over the top even for Sabrina. On second thought, it's exactly on par with her everyday behavior.

She inches back as if I slapped her. "What are you talking about? Everyone in Gingerbread will be thrilled to hear about this new honor. People will vie for the title all year long. Just think about it. Instead of mistletoe and holly strewn all around town"—she rolls her eyes as she mocks my moniker right along with my sister's—"we'll have posters of the new candidates begging people to vote for them. Of course, some of us have more clout than others." She casts a pathetic glance my way. "Anyway, I'll see you here this evening. Be a little early, and make sure Graham is here in plenty of time before dinner. I want the photographer to get a few extra pictures of the two of us." She gives a single nod, her demented gaze locked over mine. "You really are a miracle worker, Missy. Not only do I get credit for saving that ridiculous pie factory, but I get to be engaged to the most eligible bachelor this side of New York City. Graham and I are finally reuniting. And it will all go off without a hitch tonight." Her eyes slit to nothing. "And if it doesn't—that little pâtisserie you run will have to find a new home. You have less than seven hours to make this happen." She leans in with a menacing scowl. "Now *scat!*"

And I do. I run like heck right out the door, into the waiting van, and speed right back to that little pâtisserie of mine that I'll own for the next seven hours tops. And after that—it's powdered sugared curtains for me.

It doesn't look as if it will be a merry Christmas after all.

The night of the community center benefit always calls for everyone to wear their Sunday best. Over the years, some of the women—Sabrina and her cohorts—have taken it over the fashionista top. I'll admit, it's fun to see all of the men looking dapper in suits and the women dressed to the glittering nines. I've secretly envied the top of the line couture dresses Sabrina has worn proudly—a tad too proudly—in seasons past. But as for me, I've donned the very same dress for the past few years, a festive red fitted shift that hugs my curves in all the right places. No one seems to mind that the dress is on repeat, and if they do, they haven't bothered to complain about it. I primp and prime myself with the best of them for all of fifteen minutes. I've been on my feet at the bakery all day, and, to be truthful, the only thing I want to do tonight is sit by a crackling fire with Graham and Noel. Maybe I'll throw in a couple of cups of cocoa and some homemade marshmallows, too. Now that sounds like a perfect Christmas Eve if you ask me—one that doesn't include a creature by the name of Sabrina Jarrett.

But Sabrina isn't my only problem this evening. Noel proved to be a challenge to place while the entire town is gathering en mass for a Christmas feast. Graham finally found a ranch hand who readily volunteered to watch her for the evening since he needed to be home with his very pregnant wife. I'm just hoping that Noel, in all her exuberance, doesn't throw the poor lady into an early labor. It wouldn't be the first bit of mischief that baby girl has thrown herself into. And a delivery room is the one place Noel doesn't belong.

Since Graham is coming from the orchard, we've decided to go ahead and meet at the community center. He hasn't seen me yet in my tight little quasi-Mrs. Claus outfit, and God knows I can't wait to lay eyes on Graham Holiday in a suit. As much as Sabrina insists on ruining this night for me, I can't help but feel a bit elated as if Graham and I were about to attend some formal romantic venue, like say, *prom*.

My stomach tenses in knots as I head into the community center, already bustling with life. Graham might look like a dream come true, but no thanks to Sabrina that dream will be *her* reality if she can help it.

My fists ball up, and a spiral of anxiety rockets through me. All I have to do is ask Graham to sit next to Sabrina for a few hours. That shouldn't be too hard. But then, what happens next? We can't go on like this forever, can we? I know that Graham loves me. He told me so himself, and I will never forget how he looked washed in the moonlight, his eyes on fire all for me. But would he really go on with some fake relationship, for who knows how long, just so I can keep the cookies rolling in Gingerbread? I think not. It's going to take more than just a miracle or two to untangle myself from this Jarrett-shaped knot. Face it—Sabrina has me by the jingle bells, and I may never get out of this mess with my head *or* my business intact.

The room is alive with boisterous chatter and laughter as the band plays "Rockin' Around the Christmas Tree". I spot Mom speaking with a couple by the kitchen, so I head in that direction to say hello. The woman she's with turns my way, and I freeze. It just so happens the couple Mom is happily chortling away with is Samantha and Ron Holiday, Graham's parents. *Gah!* She's probably already spilled the relationship beans. No matter how much I protest, my mother is already planning our wedding. And if Sabrina gets wind of it, she might be planning my funeral, too. My feet pivot as I attempt to get lost in the crowd. All of Gingerbread has donned their finery, and I haven't even had the time to properly admire it.

"*Missy*!" Mom cries. "Oh, Missy? *Yoo-hoo*!"

I'm dead.

I turn slowly and force a smile as I head that way and quickly wish the Holidays a merry Christmas.

Mom pulls me in. "The Holidays were kind enough to extend an invitation to their home tomorrow evening. It looks as if we'll be celebrating Christmas together like one big happy family!" She looks to Samantha—Graham in female skin. "They're quite serious, you know."

"Mother!" Before I can properly refute her theory—even though she is one hundred percent correct—Holly and Tom show up with the world's most adorable little girl all decked out like a living doll. "Savanah Joy!" Mom beams as all of our attention is quickly turned to the tiny princess in a red tartan dress, and I make a break for it.

"Not so fast!" Holly chases me down and spins me around. I can't help but notice how gorgeous she looks in a matching red tartan dress to that of Savy's. If I ever have a daughter, I will most certainly subject her to that long-standing Winters' tradition that requires the younger of the Winters heirs to subject themselves to a strict lookalike dress code to that of their mother's. "Sabrina Jarrett just accosted me in the parking lot. She said something about Graham and a crown and the fact our bakery would be hers by morning if she didn't do the pageant wave before midnight." Her lips are pulled back in a scowl as she grits the words through her teeth. "Why do I get the sneaking suspicion you know exactly what that loon is referring to?" She sucks in a quick breath as she comes to an abrupt realization. "You promised her she could have Graham, and now she's going to eat our lunch! And our breakfast and our cookies, too!"

"You catch on fast." I smirk into the crowd, half-afraid I'll catch a glimpse of the wicked witch herself. But I don't. Instead, I lock eyes with a handsome prince, and I couldn't be more pleased. As harried as this night might be, there is something soothing about looking into Graham Holiday's ocean blue eyes. "I gotta run! Say a prayer it all works out! Say twelve!" I thread through the tangle of limbs until I'm locked in an embrace with the handsomest man in the room. Graham Holiday looks like a dream—my dream. His hair is glossy, still slightly damp from the shower, his cologne is strong enough to let me know that the special occasion called for an extra splash, but that Italian fitted suit, those cobalt blue eyes—my, how every last inch of me approves.

"You look"—he shakes his head while holding me out for a better view—"simply amazing."

"And you look as if you might be crowned king in just a few hours." I give a little shrug just as the music cuts out and everyone is asked to take their seats so we can say a blessing over our meal.

Graham takes me by the hand and begins leading me toward the table with Holly and her family, and we find

Tanner seated with them as well.

Sabrina steps into our line of vision, and we both freeze solid—for very different reasons, I suppose.

"Actually"—I take a deep breath—"you'll be seated in a very special place tonight." I traipse him over to the front and plant him in the spot where Sabrina all but threatened to slit my financial neck a few hours ago. I lean in and whisper to that drop-dead gorgeous, yet bewildered face. "Just play along. I'll explain everything later, I promise."

I scuttle back to Holly's table and take a seat next to Tanner. They share the same jarring blue eyes and dimples, and if I squint real hard, I can almost fool myself into thinking it's Graham himself. Almost. And I'm beginning to think the only fool around here is me.

Sabrina takes her seat next to Graham, and he shoots me a look that suggests I'll have to explain things a lot sooner than I was hoping.

The microphone picks up feedback as Mayor Todd takes the podium, and never in my life have I been so glad for the distraction.

"Welcome and good evening." He chortles while extending a cup of eggnog to the crowd. "Merry Christmas to one and all—and to one and all a merry Christmas!" He does his best impersonation of Santa while ho-ho-hoing through his laughter, and the room breaks out with a choir of Christmas greetings in reciprocation. "First, I want to thank all of the hardworking people who banded together to pull off yet another Christmas spectacular here at the community center. As you know, there will be an ongoing silent auction all evening, commencing at eight o'clock. So please open your hearts and your wallets, as all proceeds go directly to the community center itself." A polite round of applause breaks out, and Sabrina turns and hisses something at him. "Uh, yes." He clears his throat as he looks back at the crowd with a hint of apprehension. Wow, it looks as if Sabrina might have Mayor Todd by the jingle bells as well. "This evening, for the very first time, the Jarrett Foundation, which has made many generous donations to the community center over the years, has suggested we mix things up a bit." He says that last part laden with uncertainty. "Ladies and gentlemen, I want to introduce to you our very first Christmas king and queen, Sabrina Jarrett and Graham Holiday."

The room breaks out into a riotous applause as if people actually approved of this ludicrous tomfoolery. I don't even like the word *tomfoolery*, and yet with Sabrina's latest shenanigans, it fits oh so well.

Tanner barks out an obnoxious laugh as his brother reluctantly stands—or more to the point, as Sabrina yanks him from his seat. All the while Graham looks my way in what appears to be a cross between begging for help and threatening to get even. It seems old habits do die hard.

Holly yanks me in. "What the heck is happening? And

why did Sabrina just hijack Christmas and turn it into a homecoming dance?"

I wince because, truthfully, I hate that I'm in the know on this one.

"I think she just likes the attention." I clap along with the rest of the crowd as the two of them are bestowed sparkling crowns. My God, they look as if they cost some serious money. *Hey*? If Sabrina really does triple our rent, maybe I can convince Graham to cash in his crown to help chip in?

Sabrina leans into the microphone, her body doing its best to spill out of that gold lame number she's stuffed herself into like a sausage. And really? Gold lame? Has she no real friends?

"Hello!" She does that twisted wrist motion wave that she's been craving to toss our way for who knows how long. "I just want to thank everyone who came out to see us. You're in for a lovely evening. My fiancé and I are privileged to be charter members of such an exclusive club—the very first official king and queen of Gingerbread!" Graham tips his head back, and the crown nearly skids right off his head. He looks unamused by her panache to exaggerate their current relationship status, and who could blame him? The audience gives a hooting round of applause. Clearly, the eggnog is spiked this year. "Please be aware that you, too, will be eligible to run for the honor come next December, but"—she gives a cheesy wink to Graham as she takes up his hand—"have fun trying to beat this good-looking couple!" A light titter circles the room, and I'd like to think people are laughing at her, not with her. They finally take their seats, and Mayor Todd gives the official blessing over our feast. The room lights up with a thousand conversations barreling ahead at once as the band starts in on "Jingle Bells". It's a potluck, and there are three different food stations set up, so no one ever has to wait in line very long.

I stand with the rest of the table, and Tanner leans in. "You can say a lot of things about Sabrina Jarrett, but she sure saved our behinds this year."

"Oh, right, with the pies." That *I* baked. That my mother helped cultivate into the superstars they're going to be with that little pop quiz she threw me. Without the Winters women, Sabrina Jarrett is a bag of hot air. And right about now, I wish she'd float away.

Graham speeds in this direction with Sabrina by his side. The look on his face looks more like a warning of dire things to come rather than that swoony love-struck look I've grown accustomed to.

"No, no, no," I say as I bolt to the kitchen. Look busy. *Stay* busy. And for God's sake, avoid, avoid, *AVOID* those people out there tonight!

And I do, for the most part. Every now and again, I spot Graham scouring the crowd, but Sabrina has him on lockdown pretty much. Once dinner is through, and I'm pretty sure Graham didn't eat a single bite—Sabrina links her arm through his and locks him in like a vise. Every time I look over at him, he's trying to tear that crown off his head, but the wicked queen won't let him.

Bodies are circulating the side tables where the hundreds of auction items are laid out for display. I can't help but note that my gingerbread dollhouse is brimming with admirers. Let's hope at least one of them feels the need for four feet of gingerbread to take over their living room. It's so heavy, it took all of the staff at the bakery to move it. I hope someone with a very strong husband is willing to purchase it tonight.

"*Boo*!" someone whispers directly in my ear from behind, and I jump three feet in the air, only to turn to find my deviant of a sister laughing maniacally.

"It's Christmas!" Her eyes round out as if delivering earth-shattering news. "What are you doing holed up here? Savy's been asking about you all night. She's worried sick that you got lost. You've got to get back out there. You don't want to ruin her Christmas, do you?"

When the going gets tough, Holly often invokes Savanah. It's the ace in her deck for many a situation. And after witnessing how expertly she wields a hand, it almost makes me want a baby so I can play the very same game. The thought of Graham and me adding a human addition to our brood one day makes me dizzy with glee, but then I remember he probably won't be speaking to me after tonight's royal fiasco, and therefore, all talks of procreation are swiftly wiped off the table. I bet he or she would be beautiful, though, bright blue eyes, dimples, his dark hair. I wouldn't mind if that child looked nothing like me, so long as I could cuddle with that miniature version of Graham every single day.

Holly grunts as if reading my mind. "Stop your daydreaming. We've got reality to tend to," she says, speeding me back into the crowd.

The lights have dimmed just a notch, and couples are dancing on the makeshift dance floor. Then I see them—Sabrina and Graham swaying to the rhythm like a real couple. Her arms are latched over his back, and she's looking lovingly into his eyes. He laughs at something she tells him, and my stomach takes a nosedive. Nobody instructed him to have a good time. Apostate.

Sabrina yanks him down by the back of the neck and plants a firm kiss right over his lips.

I suck in a quick breath. "*No!*" I whimper. Those lips belong to me, and she's gone too far. I take a step in that direction and then recall the fact the land beneath the bakery belongs to the Jarretts, and everything in me sags. It looks as if I'm in for a lifetime of watching those two lock lips, unless of course...

Graham pulls away abruptly, and from the looks of it, he's exchanging curt yet gentle words with her. Sabrina takes a staggering step back, her eyes bulging unnaturally. It's clear she's repulsed and highly ticked off at the small dose of reality he just fed her.

"Oh no," Holly moans. "I think he just popped that airheaded balloon you've been trying to keep in the air all month. You'd better go over and straighten this out." She does her best to transport me there herself just as Nick pops up between Sabrina and Graham.

"What's going on?" he asks as if it were any of his business. He narrows his eyes on me as if what was happening between the two of them were somehow my fault. It is, but that's not the point.

Sabrina lets out a harrowing shriek. "I'll tell you what's going on. This lunatic"—she gives Graham such a violent shove to the chest half the dance floor clears out—"has professed his undying affection for that idiot!" She points a finger hard in my direction.

"No." I shake my head, trying to refute it, and I'm pretty sure I'm just making things worse by doing so.

Sabrina takes a few stomping steps in my direction, and the band quiets down a notch before stopping the music altogether. "You promised you'd give me Graham Holiday's head on a platter! You swore you were the premier matchmaker of all of Gingerbread, and I believed you! Once that gorgeous man waltzed into town, you said we were a match made in heaven."

I give a nervous glance to Graham, and our eyes lock in one horrific moment. "That's not exactly how it went." It is, but once again, that is not the point.

She tosses her hands in the air. "And then you said he would be mine by Christmas! You promised me that! I had your word." She growls out that last part as if she has suddenly morphed into a lion. "And now I find out the two of you are in *love*?" She says *love* as if it were the vilest concept known to all of man.

A light gasp breaks out around us.

Nick steps forward, pinching his eyes shut a moment. "They're not in love. Graham told me so himself. They're just friends. He assured me himself that he could never see himself ending up with my sister."

My mouth falls open as I look to Graham. He shakes his head slightly, but judging by that sheepish grin, I bet he used that line on my brother. He doesn't mean it, does he?

"Well"—Sabrina digs those daggers she calls eyes into mine—"what says you, Miss Pâtisserie?" She bears into me with her fangs, and I know exactly what her twisted little heart is getting at. "Do you love Graham Holiday?"

I give a quick glance to Holly, Tom, and little Savy who have all gathered around with long faces, trying to understand what this disruption is about. If I say yes, it will be the end of many things, starting with the bakery. And just like that, our lives will unravel one unpaid bill at a time. I glance to Graham who looks just as confused as anyone else here. His brows are doing that vexingly sexy hard V, and it's all I can do to not burst into tears. He's always been far too handsome for someone like me. I'm sure once this nightmare is over—once his vacation in Gingerbread is over, he'll forget me as soon as his plane hits the stratosphere. Can I really risk losing the bakery over something that's not even a sure thing?

Graham takes a deep breath. "I'll answer for her."

My lips press white as I try to keep from vomiting up the truth.

He clears his throat as he looks to Sabrina. "Missy isn't in love with me. The truth is, she's out of my league. Always has been." He gives a sad glance my way before reverting back to the queen of mean. "In fact, I'm leaving day after next. And I don't think either of you has to worry about seeing me again."

Sabrina looks to me with venom shooting out of her eyes. "Is it true? You don't love him?" Her jowls move from side to side. I'm sure she'll have that nipped and tucked once she reviews the footage from this evening. The entire night is recorded for posterity. Or in my case, to commemorate my spectacular downfall. "Say it!" she shouts so loud the entire room reverberates with the sound of her voice.

Nick steps in and nods for me to do it. I glance to Holly who shakes her head no, and lastly I look to Graham.

"Come on, Sprig." He nods my way, the look of hurt hiding out in his eyes. "You know we were just fooling around. I've got an entire harem waiting for me back home. You'll always be Nick Winters' kid sister to me." He swallows hard as if he wanted to say more, but couldn't bring himself to do it. "That's it."

That's it?

"Well?" Sabrina gives a slow blink as if she's losing patience with me.

"I don't." I shake my head as if refuting the claim. "There. I said it." I glare at Graham for taking it down a notch when he didn't have to. That is, unless he meant it. And if he did, I hate him for it. "I guess I don't love you after all," I say it first because with Graham I always did like to draw first blood. It's a protective mechanism I'm used to around him. And just like that, my heart shatters all over the room, and all I see is red.

I run out of the community center, hop into my car, and just start driving.

I can't go home. I'm in too close of a proximity to the enemy.

And oddly enough, it's not Sabrina Jarrett.

Graham

What the heck just happened?

I pant breathless as I watch the taillights from Missy's car disappear into the night. An impulse tells me to jump into my own truck and track her down, but something far more persistent says *get back in there and get to the bottom of the madness that ensued tonight.* There's no way Sprig wanted to see me seated next to Sabrina, did she? And that odd exchange at the end? I got the distinct feeling she didn't want to admit that she loved me for far more reasons than the fact her brother was standing right there. I played along, but I'll admit, toward the end, it didn't feel as if either of us was playing. It was hard, and I hated every minute. Worst of all, I have no clue if I did or said the right thing. Deep down, I know I didn't. I shouldn't have stooped to whatever level Sabrina was forcing us to. Sprig and I love each other, and we always will. I just hope she's feeling something far more than platonic with me. Sprig and I have never been good at being just friends. I think that alone is what spurred on the banter all these years. We wanted something more—and the one time we achieve it, some scary woman with a crown goes and ruins it for us. This can't be happening, and yet it is.

A body blows past me and turns around a moment as they hit the parking lot. It's Nick in all his ticked off glory.

"Dude"—he backtracks my way with a look that suggests he's about to rip my face off—"I will deal with you later. I told you—*told* you not to mess with my sister." He takes a few more aggressive steps in my direction. "And really? Sabrina Jarrett?" He shakes his head, not bothering to hide his disappointment in me. "I guess you're still messing with the wrong girls. Looks like you got tangled in a web you want no part of. I'm betting you wish you sat this Christmas out like you did the rest of them. Maybe you'll do us all a favor and sit the next five or ten out, too." He jumps into his truck, and I stand there absorbing his harsh words as the snow from his tires washes over me. My heart thuds over my chest as if it just lost its fervor to keep on beating, and in a way, it has. I head back in with an unwilling heart, but before I track down Missy, I need to know what I'm truly up against.

The music in the community center has picked back up. The roar of laughter and a dozen different conversations filters through the air as I amble my way back in. I crane my neck over the crowd, looking for Holly or Sabrina herself. Although, I'd much rather speak with Holly. She and Missy are close, and if anyone understands what happened here tonight, it's her. I spot Tom and Savanah by the overgrown gingerbread house, but no luck with Holly. Mom waves to me with wild eyes toward the back of the facility, and for a fleeting moment, I pretend not to see her. My God, my parents. As much as I hate how visceral everything was, I also can't stand that we had a cloud of witnesses.

Just as I'm making my way through the tangle of bodies, I spot a blonde flame of hair near the kitchen, looking like it could be Missy's sister, and it is. I make a beeline after her, and as soon as her eyes latch to mine, her mouth rounds out in horror.

"What just happened?" I move like a lion out to trap its prey as I corner her near a stack of boxes brimming with wrapped gifts for Santa to distribute in just a few minutes.

Holly moans as she drops her face in her hands. "I told her she was wrong." She looks at me through her fingers a moment before dropping her arms. "When you showed up in Gingerbread, the two of you picked up right where you left off." She swats me over the arm. "Now, why did you have to go and do that? I've known the two of you were right for one another for years. I even suggested Missy ask you to her prom."

I back up a notch as I try to digest the idea. A slow smile comes to me. "Really? That would have been great."

"Oh, I know it would have been great, but nobody listens to me!" She tosses her hands in the air in an act of outrage. "And you know what? Missy didn't even follow through with her instincts when she so ruefully decided to pair you with Sabrina." She slaps a hand over her mouth, and my stomach plummets with the revelation.

"So it's true. What made her think Sabrina Jarrett would be my perfect match?" I wince as I look out the opened door to our left at the dark cold night. Had I become so repugnant to Missy that she felt my perfect bookend was someone as shallow as Sabrina?

"Because you were tormenting her per usual!" Holly's voice rises to its upper octave before she shrinks a little as if she didn't want any part in what comes next. "Sabrina might have been holding a rent hike over our heads for months. And if you and Sabrina fell in love—who knows? She might have jet set her way to Manhattan with you. Anyway, as soon as Missy suggested you to Sabrina, she was all over it. And then, well, Sabrina became smitten with you, and so did my sister."

Everything in me warms just hearing those words. "Smitten, huh?" My spirit soars at the thought. "So, what was all that bull she was slinging in there?"

Holly slaps her hands to her cheeks. "I have no idea what possessed her to say those things. The only thing I can guess is that she's really afraid of the fallout with the bakery." She shivers as she struggles to warm her arms with her hands. "The truth is, if Mr. Jarrett decides to triple our rent— to raise it by three *cents*, the bakery is doomed." She sags as she casts a glance to the floor. "If I had to guess, it's because Missy didn't want to bring that kind of financial destruction on any of us." She looks to me as tears glide down her face.

"The bottom line is, if Sabrina Jarrett doesn't get what she wants, the bakery is burnt toast."

"And what she wants is me." I pull Holly into a partial embrace. "I'll find Tom and send him in."

"Thanks. Oh, and Graham?" she shouts after me, and I backtrack. "Missy does feel as if this entire thing between the two of you is too good to be true. Maybe you can assure her it's not? That is, if you truly feel that way."

"I do." I can't help but grin. I do love Mistletoe Winters, and I'm about to make sure everybody knows it. I head over to the stage and hop up as the band enters into "We Wish You a Merry Christmas," and I swipe the mic from the lead singer.

"Sorry," I say into it, and my voice echoes around the room as the rest of the band cuts out. The crowd gives a simultaneous gasp as they look to me in horror. "I promise this will take less than a minute. But I have to apologize for that public display you had the misfortune to witness. I feel bad that I hijacked any of your time tonight." Mom and Dad surge forward through the crowd, and I spot Tanner to my left, right along with Sabrina, who looks white as a sheet as if her life were passing before her eyes. And she's right, something is dying—our fake relationship. "I want everyone here to know that while I've been in Gingerbread, I fell in love with a spectacular girl, and it caught me off guard." Sabrina instantly brims with a greedy smile. Her hand presses to her chest as she breathes violently in and out. I'm guessing she's about to get a little more violent in a moment when she hears the rest of what I have to say. "And that girl unfortunately was being blackmailed into staying away from me."

The entire room gasps in horror, and that smile glides right off Sabrina's face.

"But that's not how love works. You can't force someone into feeling something that they don't." I look right at her as I say it. "It doesn't mean you're unlovable or that you're a bad person, it just means they're not the right one for you. And I also know that love makes you do crazy things—especially when you feel threatened. But the wrong thing to do is turn around and threaten another person and their livelihood. It's not okay, and I will not tolerate it." I spear Sabrina with a look as she shrinks toward my brother. I glance out at the crowd and find Holly with her husband, Joy and Jack Winters by their side. "I want everyone in here to know that I'm in love with Mistletoe Winters." I look to her parents with a sheepish smile, to her sister whose face is washed in tears. "There's no one else for me. That's all—and I hope you enjoy the rest of your evening. Merry Christmas." I hand the mic back to the lead singer and hop off the stage.

Holly and her mother practically tackle me, and as I welcome their riotous embrace, I can't help but notice Tanner is embracing someone, too, a sobbing Sabrina

Jarrett.

"I'm so happy for you!" Joy Winters cries out as she pinches my cheeks as if I were a little boy. "Welcome to the family. You know that I've loved you like a son for years!"

"That's very sweet of you." I'm quick to detangle myself. "I'll be right back."

Holly stomps her foot while growling at her mother. "Now look what you did! You scared him off!"

"*Tanner*!" I shout as he and Sabrina start heading toward the exit. They turn around, Tanner looking his usual ticked self and Sabrina red-faced and teary. "*Wait*." I pause a moment to catch my breath. I have no idea how to ask the question, so I just dive in. "Sabrina, did you threaten Missy's business if I didn't fall in love with you?"

Her mouth opens, and a series of croaking noises escape as she grapples for words. "Listen, I alone am the reason she still has that business to begin with. My father has been insistent on raising their rent for years, and I've singlehandedly stopped him each and every time." She looks to my brother with a smug little grin. "I'm practically a hero."

Sabrina Jarrett is a lot of things, a hero she is not.

"Hero, huh?" I sigh as my gaze drifts out the door and into the dark, dark night. I certainly don't feel like a hero. I pull out my phone, my fingers already twitching to call Missy. It's becoming clear now that Sabrina was a thorn in Missy's side that she was looking to get rid of, and when thorn number two popped into town—aka me—she thought she found her solution. But we found each other instead—together. And that's exactly where we should be, *together*.

Tanner steps forward as Sabrina heads outside into the icy night. "I'll make sure she gets home safely." He nods into the night. "Why don't you go find Missy and make sure she's okay?"

I can't help but scowl at Sabrina. "Why are you being so nice to her? You're not nice to anybody."

He glances her way, then back and sighs. "Because she saved the factory. It turns out, I've reached out to a few of our suppliers, and every single one of them is interested in samples. Sabrina Jarrett has been an answer to prayers all along."

A heavy sigh comes from the door, and we look to find Sabrina shivering. "Fine," she hisses as if talking to herself. "Missy may have had a little more to do with it than I first let on." She growls over at me, "But she let me have that idea in order to impress you. It was strictly her doing. In no way did I steal anyone's bad pie concept."

Tanner inches back. "What about those suggestions at the factory? The new uniforms to boost moral? Christmas music in the dining hall? The mural on the side of the building with the company logo?"

"All mine," Sabrina beams with pride. She steps in close to Tanner. "And I still think delivering them in a mini wooden crate would be a great idea, too."

My brother looks to me and nods. "I looked into it, and I can get them at a decent price."

"It sounds great." I can't seem to get enthused about any of this, though.

Sabrina jumps into my brother's arms. "I have a few I can bring over tomorrow. That is, if the offer still stands."

"What offer?" I'm suddenly deeply concerned for my brother.

He looks to me with those sad eyes and slowly a guilty grin emerges. "I invited her to dinner. I figured if the two of you were dating, it was a no-brainer, but now that you're not"—he looks to her—"the offer still stands. You can be my guest."

"Oh, thank you!" She hops up and offers him a kiss right on the lips. It's safe to say her Holiday plans are still up and running full throttle—only this time I'm not the Holiday in question.

"I guess I'll see the two of you tomorrow." I step out into the ice-cold night and wonder if I'll ever see Missy again. Judging by this heaviness in my heart, it may not be an answer I want to hear.

I drive for an hour, making a loop to the bakery, to her

home, and back to the bakery in the event I missed her in the interim. I called and texted before I left, and she didn't pick up, didn't respond in any way. At this point, it's clear she has no intention of being found—at least not by me. So I just keep driving until I end up at the tree lot and pull in next to Nick's truck. I hop out and spot him on a ladder taking down the sign.

He looks over his shoulder at me. "Go away. We're closed."

"I guess I'm the last person you want to see."

"You guessed right." He hops down from the third rung, wincing as he wipes the sweat from his forehead. "And I bet you're looking for my sister."

"I am, but you were next on the list of people I wanted to speak with."

Nick strides forward, his jaws set tight, still clearly ticked as ever. "Get it over with, dude. And make it quick before we both freeze."

"I love your sister." There. I said it, no warm-up, no warning.

He closes his eyes and bucks as if I shot him point-blank. "Why?" He comes up for air and glares my way.

"Why not?" I pick up a stray pinecone off the ground and chuck it over the trailer. "Missy is everything I've ever wanted. She's perfect." My heart aches because I'm afraid a part of her perfection is decoding the fact I may not be perfect for her.

"She's not your type." His chest flares out as if he's still up for a fistfight. "You like 'em fast and loose and out of your bed by morning."

"That's not me anymore. It hasn't been for a long time." I take a few steps out and stare up at the sky. I hate that it was me for so long.

"Yeah, right. Until the next woman you stumble upon."

"That's not happening," I snap. "There's just one woman for me, and it's Missy." I meet up with his heavy stare. "Nick—you're more of a brother to me than Tanner ever was. You know I wouldn't treat your sister like that. You have to believe me."

Nick glances toward the woods and lets out a roar. "Why did it have to be *my* sister?" He shoves me hard in the chest and sends me stumbling back a good six feet. "You could have had any other girl in this entire *state*!" His voice ricochets off the mountain. "Did I piss you off last year? Is this some vendetta to get back at me for not returning a phone call? What the heck were you thinking?"

A thousand thoughts sail through my mind, a thousand different ways to convince him that Missy is the one for me— and yet I doubt he wants to hear any of it, so I turn to leave.

"Where are you going?" he shouts after me.

"Anywhere but here."

"Stop." Nick jogs over, and I turn to find him grimacing

as if he were in pain. "Do you really have feelings for my sister?"

"Yes," I say, exasperated. "I love her. And if she'll have me, I'm going to marry her. I don't want to waste another second without her in my life. Tonight has made me realize that." A rush of adrenaline grips me, and suddenly I feel as if I could lap the circumference of the earth twice at least to prove this to Missy.

Nick sags as if he were defeated, and I wish he wouldn't see it that way. "Okay."

A flare of hope goes off in me, but I'm slow to get happy. "Okay? As in you're okay with this?"

"Yes." He slaps the back of his neck. "I'm going to live." His frown slowly morphs into the idea of a smile. "So if she says yes, you're legally going to be family." He comes over and slaps me on the back. "You've always felt like family to me, man."

"Same here." I give him a light sock to the arm. "Thanks for not giving me a black eye."

"I'm saving that for Christmas morning, sweetheart."

I belt out a laugh. "If you tell me where your sister is, I might just let you."

"She's at Holly's." He shakes his head. "I'll save the black eye for some other time. So, how's this supposed to work? You think Missy will close up shop and move to New York with you? On second thought, don't tell me. I don't want to spoil my Christmas. I'll take the news when it comes."

I slap him five and pull him in. "I'll see you tomorrow."

"Good luck, man. You're going to need it."

I jump into my truck and head toward the orchard to pick up Noel. Christmas is in less than a few hours. My flight for New York leaves first thing the next morning. My stomach grinds for a moment. How exactly is this going to work? And then, it hits me.

New York feels like a lifetime away. I don't know that I'm ever going back.

I know I'm not.

A thought comes to me. I think there's one more stop I need to make before I pick up Noel. And I'm going to need my checkbook for this one.

6

A Holly Jolly Christmas

Missy

Christmas morning never seems to lose its magic. Despite the heartache, the heartbreak I've endured, not to mention the tears I've shed—enough to soak a pillow. I still woke up with a sense of Christmas wonder.

Last night after I left the community center, I came straight to Holly's. Sure, there were other options, but staying with my brother might put me in a prime position for enduring a lengthy lecture about dating any of his friends. Nick has warned me on the topic for years and, ironically, I always assured him that his bevy of buddies were all safe from my hit list. And for the most part, they were because I knew that the only one of his friends that ever caught my eye was Graham Holiday. And as fate and geography would have it—he was in New York City, a safe distance from me and my dating net. Not to mention the fact he was beyond egotistical, and completely obnoxious to be around. We had fun bantering with one another, but as the years went by, I found him equally annoying as I did attractive. Case in point, my strong desire to pair him with an equally annoying person whom I was forced to grow up with, Sabrina. But I digress. Of course, I could have gone to my mother's last night, but she would have run me out of the house with her incessant sobbing. She loves Graham almost as much as I do. Any tears I might have shed last night I know that my mother shed at least a dozen more if not a hundred. Nope, my mother was not an option. And to be perfectly honest, I would do my best to avoid seeing her altogether today if it wasn't Christmas. So it had to be Holly's. I used my spare key and sent her a text once I arrived so that Tom wouldn't be moved to chase me around the Christmas tree with a wiffle ball bat in the event they thought I was a burglar. It would be just my luck to end up on the losing end of a plastic bat and have my head split open like a piñata.

Holly and I managed to wake up before the crack of dawn, and before we can hit the bottom of the stairs, Savanah's door creaks open.

"*Tom*?" Holly belts, no bothering to savor the virginal quiet still thick in the air. "She's up!"

And just like that, her door yawns open, the sound of an

eager child's feet pattering along the hardwood floors head in this direction, and both Holly and I wisely get out of the way.

"Merry Christmas!" Holly and I sing in unison as an exuberant Savy and a zombie-like Tom burst into the living room.

"Mommy!" Savanah screams at the top of her lungs once she sees the oversized gingerbread dollhouse with a big red bow on it. Holly and Tom hauled it in from the garage after Savanah went to bed. I told them it was a good thing it was only in there for a few hours or they would have played host to every mouse on this mountaintop. I know this for a fact because our gingerbread happens to be that good.

"It's all yours, honey." Holly scoops Savanah into a deep embrace before Savy makes the rounds to Tom and me as well.

"I love you." I dot her nose with a kiss. "Merry Christmas, baby girl. Now, get in there and open those presents!" An entire tower of shiny red and green boxes all wait for her to tackle them. Holly has made it a tradition to take the tiny gifts and wrap them in giant boxes in order to give the gift of *volume* as well. Each one of those boxes is lighter than air. I told her she'd have to start weighing them down with bricks if she really wants to throw her off. And Savy never seems to mind when she opens a box large enough to house a refrigerator, only to find a shiny new hairbrush inside because she's that easygoing. Mom says that a first child is always easygoing, and that's how nature tricks you into having another one. I say well-played, nature, well-played.

Tom and Holly settle on the sofa while I make a quick cup of coffee for the three of us. Savanah takes her time opening her gifts, one by one, playing with each toy for at least twenty minutes before moving on to the next.

"I've never seen a child with more patience in all my life," I whisper, and Tom belts out a laugh.

"She sure didn't get it from either of you. I'm pretty sure she got that from my side of the family."

Holly gifts him an elbow in the gut. "You wish. I was born patient. I had to grow up with this one, remember?"

"*Hey!*" I give Holly's foot a quick kick. "What's that supposed to mean? I'm the one that waited three years for—"

Holly holds up a hand, cutting me off. "The Tooth Fairy to bring you money for your front tooth. I know. We've all heard that story a million times. And it's not true, by the way."

"It is, too!" I kick her foot again, this time with a little Christmas spirit behind it. Each time this story surfaces to light, Holly insists on trying to debunk my version of it. I'd swear on a stack of Bibles that every word was true, and I might just do that to prove a point—on Christmas no less.

"It's not true because the Tooth Fairy happened to show up on the right night." She says *Tooth Fairy* in air quotes. "I just happened to wake up before you that morning."

I suck in a sharp breath at the implication.

"*Holly*!" I shout so loud Savy glances over for less than a microsecond, the longest she's paid attention to any of us since she began her unwrapping quest. "That's terrible! You had me thinking I was being jilted by the most coveted fairy of them all for the better part of half a decade."

"I couldn't help it. I was eight. Besides, I copped to Mom. I tried to convince her to give you another quarter, but she wouldn't budge. She said it would be a good lesson for me to learn by doing it myself."

"Hold the phone." I try to digest those words she slid by in the middle of her confessional. "You mean, I only got one lousy quarter for an eye tooth? I've always suspected the Tooth Fairy was cheap. So, what made you give it back, years later?"

"I didn't. A quarter must have rolled out of your jeans while you were sitting in bed and miraculously landed under your pillow. And the next morning when you woke up, I knew I was officially off the hook."

"You little stinker." I sniff into my coffee before taking a nice long swig. Tom laughs up a storm as if it were the funniest thing ever, and boy, is Holly ever lucky she found someone who finds her entertaining. "I wouldn't laugh if I were you," I'm quick to tell him. "I had to live with her for eighteen years, but you're stuck with her for life."

And just like that, the laughter ceases.

My phone bleats from deep within my purse, and I eye it as it sits on the coffee table. I purposefully didn't bother taking my phone up to the guest room with me last night. Once I let Nick and my mother know where I was headed, I figured all the really important people were taken care of. Noel comes to mind, and my heart hurts. How I wanted to spend our first Christmas together. Graham comes to mind, and my heart hurts ten times harder. How I really wanted to spend *our* first Christmas together, too. Technically, Graham and I have spent many Christmases together, but never as a couple. And that's honestly what I thought we were. Instead, we were a couple of morons. How could I have believed that Graham Holiday and I could have ever worked out?

I try my hardest to sniff back tears, but they just keep on coming.

"Oh, honey!" Holly wraps her arms around me tight. Savy turns around, and her joy melts into confusion. My heart sinks at the thought of dragging all of my shattered-heart drama into their living room, on this day of all days.

"Why is Auntie sad?" She scoots toward us on her knees midway through unwrapping a gift from my mother. All of the gifts from my mother are wrapped in a bright magenta foil this year. At first, I thought it was an obnoxious color that would cause bouts of blindness and delirium on Christmas morning, but with the lights from the Christmas tree softening it, the packages look almost magical. My mother always seems to know best. Just like she knew best when she spurred me to the idea to incorporate designer ingredients into those otherwise boring pies. A part of me wishes my mother were here to hold me just the way Holly is holding me now.

"Auntie's not sad!" Holly infuses her statement with as much enthusiasm as possible. Holly really would have made a great actress. She took every drama class Gingerbread High had to offer, all four years in a row. And a good thing, too, because with me as a sister, those are practically life skills for her. "She's just so happy to see you opening up your presents. Go on, open—*open*!" As soon as Savy turns away, Holly leans in and whispers, "See what you made me do? You made me lie to my only child on Christmas!"

I can't help but sputter a tiny laugh. "It's not a lie. I am more than happy to see her open her gifts." But Savanah is right. I'm beyond sad at the moment. Everything seemed to be going so great, and now everything is going so wrong—and on Christmas of all days! Oh, why couldn't it have been some silly holiday that I don't care about like Arbor Day? Leave it to Sabrina to rain down her wrath on the holiest day of the year.

My phone bleats again, then again, and before long the pinging sound is coming from another location. My sister reaches behind her and plucks her phone from the sofa table.

"It's Mom." Her lids lower as if she were afraid to say what comes next. "She says we're all invited to the Holidays' for dinner."

"No way, no how." I shake my head emphatically. "The three of you go right ahead. I'll stay here and guard the loot in the event any Christmas thieves try to make the rounds."

Holly bucks with a laugh. "You know we have never had a single theft on Christmas night in Gingerbread."

Tom lifts a finger. "Try ever."

"See?" She chortles at the idea once again. "I assure you that the toy store Santa dropped off for Savanah is safe and sound. You're coming with us."

"Give me one good reason why." I stare hard at my sister with that joyous look on her face. Sure, it's Christmas, but couldn't she show a little anger-fueled solidarity with me? Generally, when I'm in the dumps, Holly is kind enough to join me. The least she could do is hone in on those acting skills once again.

She leans in, her warm hand finding a home on my arm. "Remember last night when I came home I knocked on your door and said there was something important I had to tell you?"

"*Yes*." I tilt my head to the side, examining that mischievous look on her face. It's never a good thing when my sister starts to get impish.

"And you said leave me alone?"

I give a quick nod. Something tells me I should have gone home and holed up under my own covers. I'm not sure I like where that triumphant look is leading us.

"Well, I did." Her shoulders bounce with a shrug. Holly has always been one to take things far too literally.

"And what does that have to do with anything?"

Tom leans in, his glasses slipping down his nose. He might be a wonderful optometrist, but he insists he'll be the last to get laser surgery to correct his vision. He says he loves the look and feel that his wire-rimmed glasses afford. Holly says she doesn't recognize him half the time when he takes them off.

"Come on, Holly"—he tips his head my way—"let her off the hook already."

"What hook?" A rise of panic fills me. "Am I on a hook?" I scoot away from my sister to get a better look at her.

Holly giggles into her hands a moment before coming up for air. "You should never have taken off like that last night. You missed the real fireworks."

"What happened?" I deadpan so cold and fast Holly's eyes bug out because I think she realizes I'm going to kill her if she doesn't spill it quickly. I'm pretty sure she doesn't want Savy witness to a homicide, especially not hers.

"Okay, okay!" Her fingers flick through the air. "Graham went crazy trying to figure things out, and once he did, he took the stage. He knows that Sabrina was blackmailing you." Her eyes cut to the floor a moment. "And I know that you refused to admit you loved him because of me." Her cheeks pinch with color, a sure sign she's about to cry. She sniffs the air before continuing. "Anyway—he hopped on stage and wrestled the microphone from the lead singer of the band and whistled until he got everyone's attention."

My mouth falls open as I look to Tom. "Did it really happen like that?"

He pinches his thumb and forefinger together, letting me know indeed she's embellishing a bit. We both know Holly is famous for her propensity to exaggerate. But right about now, I like the exaggerated direction she's heading in.

"And then what happened?" I want to shake the details out of her like a piñata. Now I really wish I did stay so I could have seen it firsthand.

My sister's eyes mist up, and her lips pull into a sullen smile. "He said he loved you, Missy. He told the whole town he was in love with Mistletoe Winters."

My mouth falls open as I look to Tom, and he nods his head yes.

"Oh my goodness!" My hands cover my mouth to stifle the scream that's begging to erupt. "I can't believe this. Was Sabrina there by chance?"

They both offer up enthusiastic nods.

"Oh." It stings like a slap. I've lost the bakery. I blink

back tears. I don't know why this comes as a surprise. We were barreling in this direction for quite some time. "Well, that's just great." My voice makes it clear my enthusiasm is sorely lacking.

I fall back to the sofa as we watch as Savy opens the last of her presents. As soon as Tom and Holly get to exchanging one another's gifts, I opt to give them some privacy. I kiss Savy over the top of the head and wave as I duck out into the frozen morning air.

I don't know where I'm going, but I do know that I'm nowhere near ready to go home yet.

It's a funny thing, being alone on Christmas. Even with the radio bleating out its cheery Christmas music, the drive around Gingerbread feels more than lonely. Nature decided to bless us with a fresh snowfall overnight, leaving the trees thickly coated and the rooftops with a high loft of batting, sparkling like glitter over every last inch. I drive out to the lake and pause on the side of the road as I marvel at the brilliant blue hue of the water even with the sun doing its best to hide behind the clouds. I don't think I could ever get tired of seeing the contrast between the snow and the lake. Winter and summer all rolled into one visual for me. It's a beautiful sight, and I wish I had someone to share it with.

Memories of the day Graham and I spent here with Noel, building our very first snowman, taking pictures of ourselves as a family as if we were actually going to send it out as a Christmas card to friends, surge to the surface. It's hard to believe it took place just a little over a week ago, and here I am at the lake with nothing but a few pictures on my phone to remind me of how perfect life could be. It was perfect. Even if all Graham and I ever had was that microcosm, it was more love than most people will know in a lifetime.

I wipe the tears from my eyes as I continue down the road and take a turn onto Bloomwood Road, only to stop the car cold in the exact location where we declared our love to one another. Over the years, Graham and I have shared a lot of sentiment with one another, some of them downright colorful, but never had we even uttered the L word. It all felt so very special. The moonlight washing us with its magic, the twinkle lights on the enormous sleigh we were seated in, the sound of the carolers floating up from a distance. It felt as if we left reality and fell into a Christmas greeting card. It was all so perfect, so magical—deep down, I wondered if it was too good to be true.

I force myself to drive on and head straight to the end of Main Street with its giant decorated tree, the lights still on and the star on top as bright as ever. This right here is where Graham and I shared a delicious, steamy kiss. I knew when it happened that it was a moment I would remember for the rest of my life. I thought for sure he would, too. Kissing Graham in the middle of town, in front of the tree we grew up venerating year after year felt like a milestone—a blessing.

My lungs fill with an extra-large breath as I sit mesmerized by the overgrown evergreen. I wonder how it will feel to be here next year looking at this beautiful tree knowing the secrets that it's harboring? Graham was my first kiss in what feels like forever, but he also delivered the best kiss that I've ever had. My body aches as I think of the memory. Holly said he declared his love for me in front of everyone at the community center. Graham loves me, and he made sure to tell every last person in that room, including one too many Jarretts. A fire of both dread and elation rips through me at the thought as I head toward the bakery.

The bakery. I sit out front, just looking at the cute pink box of a building with the giant gingerbread cookie as its sign. Holly thought it would get the point across quickly if we used a gingerbread man. That way people who were in a hurry and didn't have time to read the words *Bakery and Café* would still get the gist. Holly has been great at marketing, and an even better business partner. I wouldn't change anything we've done with this place.

"It was fun while it lasted," I whisper as I let myself inside. The lights are all off, and the entire establishment looks darn right depressing with just the blue cast of natural lighting streaming in from the windows. I head over and flick on every light in the house, something I never do when I'm here early to bake. Holly and I always reprimand one another if we do. Holly figured out that we'd have to sell at least a dozen extra cookies to pay for overused electricity, and hustling cookies is hard enough as it is. I pause as I walk by the refrigerated cases, the glass cases, that the customers get to browse through as they make their selections. At the moment, every cupboard is bare. Holly and I are big on putting all of our inventory away at night in airtight tubs. That way, even if we do sell a day old cookie, we're still confident that it's fresh as can be. But looking at the arid spaces where our happy goodies nestle during the day, it just brings me down another notch or twelve. There's something so sad about empty shelves. Usually I bypass them in the morning without thinking twice, but knowing that they'll most likely never be filled to the brim again makes my heart ache.

I make a fresh pot of minty mountain cocoa and head to the kitchen, to the enormous slab of white Carrara marble that Holly and I picked out ourselves at the quarry. I run my hand along it and try to memorize how soft and cool it feels. Even though marble is rock solid, the counter has always felt like velvet to me—most likely because it forever has a film of flour over it. I switch on the ovens without thinking and smile.

Hey? Maybe baking something is just what the doctor ordered. I need to get my head around what happened last night. And what happened after I left was even stranger. I'm thrilled to hear that Graham still loves me, but I happen to know firsthand that he leaves for New York in the morning. How is it possible that I'm about to lose two things that I love so dearly? The bakery *and* Graham.

Boy, one would think you'd have to break a mirror every day of the week for an entire year to have that kind of luck. Not me, though. I somehow managed it effortlessly.

I pull out every pan and bowl in sight, every ingredient known to mankind, too, still stymied as to what I might make—on this, what will most likely be my final foray in baking in this precious kitchen. I'm just about to pull out the flour when the bells attached to the front door rattle out their sweet refrain.

Great. I forgot to lock the door behind me. I bet it's Sabrina looking for scraps before she gives me the big heave-ho.

"Sorry, we're closed!" I shout just as I round the corner and come face to face with the most gorgeous man in all of Gingerbread—New York City or the world.

Graham offers up a sheepish smile and holds out a bright red box with a gold bow on it. "Merry Christmas, Missy," he says it soft as he holds the gift out between us like a peace offering. But I can't seem to take my eyes off those blue eyes and dimples. "You think I can hang around even though you're not open?"

A thought occurs to me and sends my adrenaline soaring through the ceiling.

"Where's Noel?" I ask in a panic in the event he's left her outside to freeze in the snow. It might be her favorite thing to do, but it doesn't mean it's good for her.

"With my parents. I had breakfast with them this morning, and they were happy to watch her while I stepped out. I had a very important delivery to make."

"In that case." I make a face before a full-on smile takes over. "I think there's room for one more. Merry Christmas, Graham." I tick my head for him to follow me to the kitchen, and he does.

"You look beautiful." He comes in close, sliding the gift on the counter my way.

"I'm wearing my sister's sweats. I'm not even sure they're clean, but thank you." My face heats like an oven set to broil. I can't seem to take my eyes off of him. Graham Holiday looks resplendent in his red checkered flannel, his dark inky jeans. I love Graham in a suit—I'd be crazy not to—but there's just something about him in a flannel that gets my heart racing to unsafe levels, and I love the rush he gives me. It's safe to say I'm addicted to it.

"This is for you." He eyes the gift.

"Oh, thank you. I, um, don't have anything for you at

the moment."

He shakes his head as if I were missing the point. "Go ahead and open it. I think you might like what's inside." He shrugs, and the dimples in his cheeks dig in deep. "At least that's what I'm hoping."

"Well, if it's from you, I'll love it." I pull it forward and glide my fingers through the tape on the sides. "Unless it's a flying snake. I never did appreciate those, you know." Graham thought it was hysterical to house a rubber snake in just about everything just to watch it pop out and frighten the living daylights out of me.

Graham belts out a laugh, and just like that, the tension in the room dissipates, melts like snow. "That was simply a tradition I had to uphold, and you know it. But I promise you no flying snakes. Not this time anyway."

"Oh!" I laugh along with him. "So I'll have to keep an eye out for it next time. I see how it goes." Next time. My heart soars at the prospect, but neither of us has said a word about last night, about the thousands of miles that will separate us starting tomorrow. I take off the wrapping, pull the lid off the box, and gasp. "Graham, no!" I land my hands over my mouth as I tremble just looking at it.

"Yes. It's all yours, Missy. My grandmother gave it to me because I'm the oldest, and I'm giving it to you because you're the wisest."

Carefully, I pull out the Holiday family treasure, his

Grandmother's prized cookbook. A gorgeous blue notebook with gilded lettering that reads *Recipes*. I leaf through it with the utmost care and marvel at the beautiful penmanship that each page harbors.

"Graham, this is a family heirloom. I don't think I can accept this."

"Too bad. It's yours. I don't take gifts back, and there are no exchanges."

I'll admit, I'm a bit terrified to hold it. It's almost the exact feeling I had when Savy was born and she was placed in my arms at the hospital for the very first time. It's so precious, fragile even. This is a cherished bit of Holiday family history, the very part that ushered in the era of Holiday Pies. And then I land on a precious page. "Pumpkin pie." I bite down on a smile as I look to Graham. "I think I know what I'd like to bake right now. In fact"—I flip the page and nod to Graham with a devious smile—"I know two things I'd like to bake."

"Great. I'll help you. We'll bring them with us tonight to my mother's annual Christmas party. Rumor has it, your family will be there, too."

"I guess we'll be going together then." I melt a little at the idea. "We'd better get baking if we want to make it on time." I set his grandmother's cookbook over to the clean counter behind me and place a large plastic sheet over the pages so I won't get any food on it while reading the recipe.

The last thing I want to do is ruin this gift that I will treasure until the day I die.

Graham helps me wash, core, and peel the apples. We get the pumpkin pie mix out and make each of the pies to his grandmother's specifications.

"I think this is a good place to stop," he announces as he pulls the pie crusts out of the oven, a buttery golden brown. I always prebake my pie crusts before adding in the filling because if you don't you just end up with an ooey gooey mess—but for sure it's not a good place to call it a day.

"What do you mean *stop*? We haven't even gotten the pies in the oven. It's a terrible place to stop. I'm pretty sure if I turn up at your mother's Christmas party with a couple of empty pie shells, your parents will hate me."

A dark laugh strums from him because he knows I'm right. "Nobody will hate you, I promise." He cranes his head to the counter behind me and winces at his grandmother's cookbook. "Least of all my grandmother."

He looks back and hooks into me with those persistent lake blue eyes. Graham Holiday has a way of making you feel as if you're the most important person in the room. That has always been my favorite part about him. Even when he was vexing me, I still felt as if I were his favorite person to vex, and now *that's* a talent.

"I don't get it. You lost me at grandmother."

"You've mixed enough of her ingredients into the pies.

Now, let's bring two Winters' originals with us. It turns out, the buyers of the local stores are all interested in sampling your ideas. Sabrina told me everything. You saved Holiday Pies, Missy. Thanks to you, the entire crew in Cater gets to keep their jobs. And not only that, there's about thirty more jobs being added to the roster."

"*Graham*!" I leap over and wrap my arms around him, pulling him into a tight embrace. Graham feels solid and warm, so very real, and my heart breaks because at this time tomorrow the only thing I'll have to hold onto is memories. I pull back and look into those watery blue eyes. "Holly told me about what happened when I left the community center last night." I wince. "I wish I was there to hear it myself. How did it go again?"

His chest rumbles with a laugh. "It went something like this"—he tips his head back and shouts—"I love Mistletoe Winters!" he belts it out for the entire neighborhood to hear.

A laugh ripples through me. "And if I was there, I would have said this"—I tip my head back, readying my vocal cords to perform at the same octave—"I love Graham Holiday!"

We share a laugh as we settle our gazes on one another.

"I really do love you, Missy." He swallows hard. "Did you really think that Sabrina Jarrett and I would make a good couple?" He tilts his head to the side, looking playfully pained.

My fingers cover my lips a moment. "I may have

thought it was a brilliant means to an end." I wrinkle my nose at the thought. "And now that you're no longer a couple, I have to give up my winning streak. It's sort of ironic that I'm no longer batting a thousand thanks to my own interference."

"Well, if it's for your record, I can always go and hunt down Sabrina."

I give his ribs a quick pinch. "Don't you dare!" I laugh at the thought. "She is a monster, though." My voice grows quiet, but I refuse to let her ruin this beautiful moment. I don't know how much Sabrina really told him. Her version of everything and reality could very well be two different things.

"I don't want to talk about Sabrina," he whispers, his eyes still pinned to mine as his head inches closer to me.

"Me either," I say as the smile glides right off my face.

Graham glides his lips over mine and kisses me right here in the bakery, in the place that has been the nerve center of my heart for the last three years. But I can officially say that it has been demoted a rung. There's a new sheriff in town that holds the key to my heart, and his name is Graham Holiday. Our kisses grow with intensity as we hold one another tight. Graham and I have somehow managed to glue ourselves together again, and all is right with the world this beautiful Christmas morning.

Graham helps me bake two exquisite, delicious designer pies, and once they're baked and cooled, we box them up. I collect his grandmother's recipe book as we leave, and I can't help but give the bakery one last forlorn look before we head out the door. And I wonder deep in my heart if that's the last time I will ever turn out the lights.

Graham

The sign above Holiday Orchards is festooned with garland, strung with lights, and has a giant red bow over the center of it the size of a refrigerator. The ground is covered in snow as far as the eye can see in every direction, and it makes the barn, the main house my parents live in, look all that much more enchanting. It doesn't take much to turn Holiday Orchards into something out of a fairy tale, but this evening it glows with an otherworldly appeal altogether. Magic lingers in the air, the very same magic that brought me to Missy.

"That's an awful lot of cars," Missy marvels as I end up parking a good distance away. I offered to drop her off at the door, but she insisted she was fine with the short hike. "There must be at least fifty people in there. I guess this is our official debut as a couple."

"That it is." I let Missy know all about my meeting with her brother last night, and she was relieved to know that there wouldn't be a knock-down, drag-out fight in front of the Christmas tree. "It might be strange for like a minute, but I'm pretty sure that will dissipate quickly. It's Christmas." I give her knee a quick pat. "People love a happy ending."

We get out, and I do my best to balance the pies as we make our way to the front door. The front of the palatial home I grew up in has lights strung on every available surface. For as long as I can remember, my mother has been a firm believer in the fact you cannot have too much Christmas. Each room in that house is covered with sentiments that represent the holiday, from the entry to the broom closet. Each room has its own miniature tree, and the living room houses one that stretches to the vaulted ceiling. It's quite a sight, and that's just the point. It's safe to say my mother has covered her Holiday territory.

I stop shy of opening the door and pause to look at Missy. "You are more than stunning tonight." We stopped off at her house after the bakery, and she changed into something she thought fit the occasion better than her sister's sweats. But in truth, Missy could have kept the sweats on and still have been the most beautiful woman in that room tonight—in all of Gingerbread. And then, of course, we sat by the fire, warming one another with our arms wrapped around each other, sharing stories from Christmases past. It's amazing to look back and see how obvious my attraction was to her. I only wish I could have realized my feelings for her sooner.

"And you look far too gorgeous to ever leave the house," she says it like a reprimand, but the corners of her lips curl up. "And I love it. Thank you for choosing me."

I inch back a notch. "Trust me, I'm the one who's grateful." I blink a smile. "I think I'm about to steal a kiss."

"Oh?" She glances up. "I don't see any Mistletoe."

"I do."

A throaty laugh bubbles from her. "That line will never get old."

I steal a quick kiss before we step into the house and shout a cheery, "Merry Christmas!"

The living room is filled with familiar faces, of family and friends, all of them standing around and mingling while Christmas music fills the air. But the one friendly face we've both been dying to see is the one bounding in our direction at the moment.

"*Noel!*" Missy falls to the floor as Noel tackles her, and they both roll around in the foyer as if they hadn't seen one another in months—*years*. Missy quickly gets on her knees as Noel licks her cheeks. "I have a present for you back at the house." She plants a kiss over Noel's forehead and springs to her feet, dusting off her knees as if it were the most natural thing in the world to roll around the floor at a Christmas party. And that's why I love Missy most—she's not afraid to just be herself. "Are you sure your mom is okay with having her in the house with so many people? So many potential shoes to gobble up?"

"Are you kidding? It's her first grandchild. She wouldn't have it any other way."

Mom and Dad step over to greet us, as do Joy and Jack Winters, and we exchange a holiday greeting with each of them.

"So?" Missy's mother beams with pride. "I take it everything is back to how it should be?" She looks from Missy to me with the excitement bubbling from her.

Missy glances my way. "Exactly how it should be. And I want to apologize for that horrible outburst at the auction last night. I hope you'll all forget about it and put it out of your minds forever." She shudders at the memory.

My mother and Joy exchange a quick glance. Finally, Mom clears her throat. "I don't think we can forget about it entirely. But I do suggest that everyone plays nice tonight." She glances over her shoulder before leaning in toward Missy. "We have a few extra guests that you might want to steer clear of."

I grunt because I may have forgotten all about the fact Tanner insisted on inviting Sabrina.

Missy stands on her tiptoes a moment until she spots the blight and sucks in a lungful of air. "Wow, I guess that's the last person I expected to see here tonight." She squints into the living room. "It looks as if she's still clinging to Tanner pretty hard." She looks to me. "Do you think she's waiting for me to alleviate her of her duties?" Missy filled me in on the plot to send Sabrina in Tanner's direction. A brilliant move if you ask me. I'd say *poor Tanner*, but judging by that ear-to-ear grin, he doesn't look too traumatized by her presence.

"Why don't we go over and find out?" I wrap an arm around her shoulders, and both her mother and mine fan themselves at the sight, giggling like a couple of schoolgirls. "Excuse us. I think it's best if we break the ice and start the night off on the right foot."

Missy and I head over to the enormous fireplace already roaring with a blazing fire. The exact fire that Tanner and Sabrina are warming themselves by.

"Merry Christmas," Missy sings, and the two of them turn to us with pleasant expressions. For the first time since I've set foot back in Gingerbread, Sabrina Jarrett doesn't look as if she's about to devour me. In fact, judging by the way she's leaning toward my brother, I'd say her sights are set in another Holiday direction.

Tanner and Sabrina each offer up a polite merry Christmas, and Tanner actually smiles at me for the first time in years.

"It looks as if Santa was good to you both," I tease as I rock back on my heels, still admiring how affable they both seem at the moment.

"Better than good." Tanner nods to Missy. "Thank you for saving Holiday Pies. Sabrina let me know it was you who worked to make those recipes."

She nods "It was my pleasure. Actually, it was my mother who spurred me on to get there. And, of course, I had a blast playing in the kitchen. It's something you'll never have to twist my arm to do. My favorite is the salted caramel apple pie, and the s'mores pumpkin. Graham came by this morning, and we baked one of each so the two of you can sample them if you like." She gives a little shrug. "I hear the local stores are interested in perusing them. That's great. I'm really happy for you, Tanner. All of you." She looks to me with a glimmer in those periwinkle eyes.

"Actually"—my brother takes in a deep breath, and I'm half-afraid he's going to take us to some dark place by telling us that the stores changed their minds—"I got in touch with a buyer from a big box store. He said farm-to-table is really big, and he loves the fact we're baking using our own fresh produce. They're interested in meeting up with us."

"What?" I pull my brother in for a quick embrace. "That's fantastic!"

Tanner winces as if maybe it wasn't. "You think you can come to the meeting with me? I can handle the small reps, but I can't afford to goof this up."

"You bet. Just let me know when and I'll be there. I plan on being around a lot more often."

Missy's eyes widen at the prospect. I haven't broken the news to her yet because it's a part of the second Christmas gift I'm going to give her tonight. But it's the third gift that I'm hoping will have her floating ten feet off the ground.

Sabrina scoffs. "You can handle that meeting alone, Tanner." She straightens the collar on his dress shirt, and

Missy and I exchange a glance. "You're the most confident man I've ever met. So what if you're a little rough around the edges? Who isn't? My favorite part about you is that you don't put on airs."

"What's going on?" Missy shakes her head at Sabrina. "Is this?" She points to the two of them. "Are you?" She leans in, unable to finish the question.

"We are!" Sabrina wraps her arms around my brother, and if I didn't know better, he looks rather happy about it. "It's official. We're *dating!*" She bounces on her heels as if she were on springs.

"Dating." I inch back and study my brother as he breaks out into a big old grin, and the sight of it warms me. "Congratulations, man." I'd warn him about her, but I'm starting to get the feeling he's dating a whole new Sabrina Jarrett. In the least, he's well aware of what he's getting himself into.

"Wow," Missy marvels, clearly stunned on her feet. "Ditto that. Huge congratulations. To many more—*dates*." She shrugs, and the four of us share a laugh.

Sabrina and Tanner excuse themselves as they head for the eggnog, and Missy steps in close to me.

"I'm not sure whether I should apologize or reclaim my perfect track record? He is a Holiday, you know." She lifts a shoulder my way, and I can't help but think she's adorable. I have always thought she was adorable, and the thought alone makes me smile.

Joy Winters steps up with Holly. "What track record?" She looks to her younger daughter.

Missy glances to my brother. "I knew I was setting up Sabrina Jarrett with a Holiday for life. It turns out, my matchmaking skills are still intact. My perfect record remains just that, perfect." She and Holly share a high five.

Mrs. Winters holds up a hand. "I believe it's my record that remains perfectly intact." She gives a sly wink my way. "I have had my fair share of perfect matches, too, you know."

"Like who?" Missy asks as if she didn't have a lot of faith in what her mother was suggesting. It's safe to say two women warring over the same track record can bring the tension to the party real quick.

"Like you." She flicks a finger between us while sipping her fruity green drink from a thin red straw. It's mint jubilee. Mom makes it every year because it looks festive, and she calls it Holly-ade. "Don't for a minute think I didn't know who would be waiting for you at that realty office that afternoon." She averts her eyes to the ceiling and gives a coy smile.

"*Mother*!" both Missy and Holly chime at once.

I can't help but shed a laugh. "So, you had Missy meet with me that afternoon?"

"I sure did." She waves a proud finger in the air. "And I may have—"

241

Noel bounds over, and Missy picks her right up. "Here's my Christmas baby."

Mrs. Todd—Rose, Mayor Todd's wife, pokes her head in our small circle for a moment. "Isn't she the best?" She looks to Joy. "You really got the pick of the litter. She had the rest of those puppies sold in a week! You came just in the nick of time, or this little precious one would have had another home by now." She gives a slight wave before melting back in the crowd.

"Mother?" Holly takes a solid step away from her.

But Missy leans in. "Explain yourself. Quickly." Her tone is curt, and neither she nor Holly takes their eyes off her. To be honest, I can't either.

"What's this about?" I reach over and land my hand over Noel's warm back, and she nuzzles into me.

"Oh, I don't know"—Joy looks to the four corners of the room before zeroing in on us. "Okay, so my wheels might have started churning after you called and said you were coming into town." She frowns at me. "I always thought you and Missy would end up together one day. The way you two bantered, it was only a matter of time. Why, you were an old married couple long before you even knew you were a couple."

Missy and I share a dull laugh.

Holly huffs at her mother. "Get to the dog."

"Well"—she winces—"no sooner did we get off the

phone than Rose called, letting me know her sister's lab had a litter of puppies, and she wanted to know if I wanted to get one for Savanah."

"Oh, man!" Holly protests. "You mean Noel could have been mine?" She looks to Missy. "We are definitely sharing."

"Anyway"—Joy continues—"I couldn't resist the idea of a puppy bringing the two of you together. And once I realized the only furnished home was next to yours, I drove over and waited until the two of you arrived, and, well—you know the rest."

Missy shakes her head in disbelief. "So that's why no one called the shelter to report a perfectly healthy missing puppy." She glares at her mother a moment before melting into a smile. "Thank you." She leans against my shoulder. "You gave me two things that day that I will forever be grateful for."

"I concur." I touch my head to Missy's. "I guess you both have a perfect track record."

"*Aw.*" Holly breaks out into a spontaneous applause. "How about I take Noel and let Savy play with her a bit?" She takes our baby right out of Missy's arms. "I think at this point in my life I like being an aunt to Noel. Tom and I already have our hands full."

Joy leans in and pinches my cheeks. "You're welcome." She gives a little wink before they both slip into the crowd.

"Well, how do you like that?" Missy stares out at the

tree, stunned. "My own mother pulled one over on me."

"And I'm glad about it, too."

She bumps her shoulder to mine. "Me, too."

I lean toward the window and wince. "What's that sound I hear? Is that sleigh bells?"

Missy laughs and swats me. "That was last night. I'm pretty sure the man in the red suit is sawing logs by now. Rumor has it, he hibernates for the rest of the winter."

"I'm betting that's what you wish you could do after that rush you had that began around Thanksgiving and ended last night."

"The bakery." She nods, looking ever so sad when she says it.

"And on that note, I think we should head out front to see if Santa left us anything." I take her by the hand as we thread through the crowd.

"Graham Holiday, what are you up to?" She bubbles with laughter all the way to the front porch, down the stairs, and under the giant pine my parents have adorned with a million little twinkle lights.

I pull a small red box from my left pocket and hand it to Missy.

"Graham?" She tips her head to the side. "What's this?"

"Traditionally the giver doesn't reveal the gift. It's up to the receiver to open it."

"Okay, smart aleck." She breaks out into an ear-to-ear

grin as she quickly tears at the paper and opens the tiny box. "A key." She looks up, momentarily confused. "Is this a key to your penthouse in New York?" Her voice hangs heavy in the air as if it were a tragedy in the making.

"No. I promise you, what this opens is as far away from New York as I'd want to be."

"Well, you don't have a house. Did I just get my very own key to the factory?"

"Strike two. But I do believe there is a note inside with the address."

She peels the tiny paper from the bottom of the box and inspects it. "2218 Main Street?" she whispers as she scans the ground as if searching for answers. "Graham, that's the address of the bakery." Her mouth opens wide as she gasps for her next breath. "Graham, what does this mean?"

"It means you don't have to worry about Mr. Jarrett raising the rent on you. I bought the building. Everyone has a price. Thankfully, Mr. Jarrett's wasn't all that high. It's true. After I left the tree lot, I went back to the community center and made him an offer he couldn't refuse. And in doing so, I closed my very first deal in Gingerbread."

"Oh my goodness, Graham!" she squeals as she wraps her arms around me for a moment before pulling back. "What do you mean, your first deal in Gingerbread?"

"I mean, the first of many. I'm not leaving, Sprig. You'd better get used to me because I'm not going anywhere."

"Oh, Graham." She grips me once again, this time with far more force. She pulls back, and her eyes dance with a playful glimmer. "I guess this makes you my new landlord." Her teeth graze over her bottom lip. "I guess I'd better ply you with all the sweet treats you can eat so I don't have another unexpected rent hike."

I shake my head. "I'm not your landlord, Missy. I'm giving you the building."

"What?"

I reach into my right pocket and drop to one knee. "In fact, I'd like to give you something else."

Her hands cover her mouth in an instant as tears begin streaming from her eyes.

"My grandmother left me one more thing. Her wedding ring. And tonight, I'd love to gift it to you. Mistletoe Winters, would you do me the honor of becoming my wife?"

"YES!" she cries out with a primal scream.

A roar of applause breaks out behind us, and we turn to find bodies spilling out of the doorway. Watching from a distance is everyone we know and love, Noel included. Nick nods over to me before giving us both a thumbs-up, and it feels official in every capacity. Missy and I are happening—we're getting married.

"Kiss her!" someone shouts, and I stand up and do just that.

Missy and I kiss right there under the moonlight, in

front of friends and family, and even Noel who scampers her way out and nips at the two of us. The crowd behind us breaks out into laughter, and another round of applause ensues.

As messy as it all may have been—we've somehow managed to find our Christmas miracle and tie a nice neat bow on it in the end.

Mistletoe Winters is mine, and I am hers.

It is a merry Christmas indeed.

And it will be a merry and bright happily ever after—I'll make sure of it myself. Together, Missy and I have all the right ingredients.

Epilogue

Missy

Three months later...

The little white church tucked in the back of Gingerbread like an afterthought is most certainly on the forefront of everybody's minds on this, the second Saturday of March. It's certainly on my mind since I'll be lost in wedded bliss in less than a few hours. Wedded bliss. My insides quiver as I think of all it entails. Today marks the start of a life with Graham Holiday as my husband, and I can't help but lose myself in trying to memorize every last detail the moment has to offer.

"Let's get inside!" Holly screams as she bustles past me along with a small army of strangers my wedding planner hired to make sure this day goes off without a hitch.

Graham wanted to hire a fancy wedding planner from New York who could make all of my wedding fantasies come true. But luckily, I stopped him before he could fly her out. It turns out that Mayor Todd's wife, Rose, her sister Ruby—the very one that sold Noel to my mother is a renowned wedding planner from Denver. Ruby has been the biggest blessing of all. Once I told her I basically had zero wedding fantasies and have never created a Pinterest board that had anything to do with matrimony, she narrowed the themes down to a few choices: rustic, classic, and fairy tale. I chose a combination of all three, which only made her shake her head. I'm pretty sure I've inadvertently turned into her most difficult client yet and simultaneously the easiest going. I've basically said yes to whatever she's suggested. I'll be just as surprised by the details as our guests will be. I already have my every dream coming true. I'm marrying Graham Holiday.

It's been a whirlwind these last three months, what with him closing up shop in New York and moving back to Gingerbread lock, stock, and barrel. I went with him twice to close out his last few deals and hire movers to pack and pedal all of his rather expensive wares clear across the country. While we were there, we took in four shows on Broadway— something he says he never took the time to do, so it was virtually new to both of us. They were spectacular, and he's officially dubbed me a theater buff, thus promising to bring me back once a year to keep up my new addiction. We ate at an Irish pub with the most delectable menu that I will never forget. Gingerbread needs an Irish Pub stat. The shepherd's pie was to *die* for. And, of course, we had deep-dish pizza in Little Italy that blew our minds. We will never breathe a word of it to the owners of Angelino's. And once we were back in Gingerbread, Graham put his things in storage and continued to rent the Spitzers' place. He only has the rental until the end of the month because they are actually coming home for the spring and summer. But Graham won't be needing their place after today because he'll be moving in with me until we can build our dream house by the lake. Graham and I knew we wanted to live in Gingerbread, and as much as I love my tiny house, it's just that, tiny. Plus, I love the thought of a fresh start. Graham and I designed every inch of our new home with an architect. Now if we could only fast-forward to the day we move in. Until then, Graham and I will be comfy cozy in my itty-bitty abode just as soon as we get back from our honeymoon. *Honeymoon*! I'm so excited about the quasi-requisite vacation that I almost forgot to bring my shoes to the church. Graham and I decided to spend an entire month in Hawaii basking in the warmth of the sun—or more to the point, the comfort of air conditioning while discovering all the interesting things to do behind closed quarters.

Holly pokes her head out of the bright blue door, and her blonde hair blows in the wind. "Missy! Get in here! We're short one bride!"

"Coming!" I give a quick wave as she ducks back into

the building. I give one final look around Gingerbread with its blue skies, the lake in the distance, snow still on the north facing side of the mountain, but the spring grass is here, along with fields of lavender, and mustard weeds with their pretty yellow sprays. If I stand on my tiptoes, I can see the evergreen on Main Street that's decorated as the town tree each year. Then if I look left, I can almost see my own neighborhood. It's the very spot where Graham and I shared our first blissful kiss. I look back at the church and take a deep breath. And that's the very spot where Graham and I will share our first kiss as husband and wife. Tears come to my eyes, and I do my best to blink them back. The world will be different—brand new again, once I step out of that church later this afternoon. It's going to be better. Much, much better.

I scuttle inside, careful not to slip on the gravel in the parking lot as I make my way to the beautiful church. As soon as I set foot inside, the floral scent of roses fills my senses. I blow past the foyer and peek my head into the sanctuary, and this time I buck with tears. I knew it would be beautiful, but this is beyond anything I could have asked for. Miles of pink old English roses and peonies are strung together like garland as they traipse up and down the pews, all the way down the aisle. A floral arch has been erected in front of the altar with a plethora of flowers draped over it, thick like a blanket. Ruby assured me a floral arch at an indoor event is all the rage back in New York and L.A., and being the amicable bride I am, of course, I agreed to it. But looking at it in person just blows my mind. I can't imagine there are any flowers on the free market left to sell. They're all right here in Gingerbread at my wedding.

"Missy!" Holly runs out of the bridal room in a robe, pink sponge curlers in her hair, and one fake eyelash attached crooked to her lid. I can't help but think she looks like she's getting ready to go trick-or-treating. "I am going to leash you to the chair!" She scuttles us over to the open door on the side of the foyer and inside it's beauty central. The makeup artist Ruby hired has fanned out all of her pastel goodies, and Savanah is knee-deep in brushes, her face glowing like a bright red light bulb.

"Savy!" Holly shrieks and takes off to help remove the pink dust from her daughter's face.

"You must be the bride!" A tall, beautiful woman with makeup so thick it looks as if she applied it with a frosting knife plunks me in what looks like a massage chair and begins manhandling my face as if it were her own. "My name is Myrna. Just relax. I'm going to make you look like a doll!"

And that's what I'm afraid of.

Ruby appears with a petite blonde by her side. "And this is Ari," she over enunciates, most likely because it looks as if I'm only paying half-attention. She would be, too, if she just had lotion slathered all over her face. "She's going to do your hair."

"Loose curls," I say in the event the makeup artist glues my lips shut. "Just something natural. I want to look like myself." I glare up at the brunette who seems to have a vendetta out on my cheeks.

A sudden breeze whooshes in just as my mother strides into the room. "Sam and I are here!" she trills, and I glance toward the door to see Samantha, my soon to be mother-in-law, traipsing in behind her. "What did we miss? What do we do? My goodness, where are our dresses?" she shrieks each word out as if there was a fire in the building.

Holly holds up a hand in my direction. "I've got this," she assures before systematically attending to my mother's panic attack. Holly promised me that she'd keep a lid on our mother and her panache for spiraling wildly out of control. On poor Holly's wedding day, Mom had a full-blown panic attack that involved the paramedics and a defibrillator.

Savanah bops over with her cute little robe and kitten heels with pink feathers wafting in the breeze. "I painted my nails." She extends a tiny little hand dotted with bright pink polish.

"I love them. You look quite elegant today." And she does. Savy is a beautiful girl any day of the week, but throw in a little primping, and she's a supermodel in the making.

"My mom says you're going to have all the fun while she pulls her hair out for two weeks." She makes a face. "And that

Noel will probably make brownies in my room and eat all of Daddy's shoes."

"She might be right—but it's actually for an entire month. You and Noel should be best friends by then. Word to the wise, hide your best boots." I wince as my sister does her best to call Savanah over.

"Hard truths on my wedding day," I shout over to her, and she gives a playful scowl. "It's true, though. Noel hasn't quite grown out of her shoe eating phase. On an up note, I think I just figured out a way to get you a whole new shoe wardrobe. And you're welcome."

Mom scoffs as the hairdresser combs out her locks. "Send her to my house next! Your father is so cheap he squeaks."

"I advise you to get a puppy of your own." I don't dare send Noel to my mother's house unsupervised. It's a well-known fact that she feeds her table scraps every chance she gets. I can't blame her. Once Noel gives you those sad brown eyes, you'll want to do anything to lift her spirits. She's a master manipulator at its finest.

Samantha chortles out a laugh. "Last week, Noel ate a hole right through Ron's golf bag. I had no idea he knew so many colorful words.

Great. My future father-in-law most likely already has a squabble with me. I don't foresee rough waters with either Samantha or Ron, though. We get together at least once a week for dinner, and they've both insisted that I call them Mom and Dad. I'll admit, it felt odd the first few times, but now it feels like second nature. The only time I seem to hold back is when my own parents are in the room.

An hour drifts by, then two, and soon I'm admiring myself in the full-length mirror in my snow-white wedding dress with its sweetheart neckline and Italian lace sleeves. My mother and Holly helped me whittle the selections down from a couple hundred to this perfect virginal dream. Holly and Mom took one look at it on me, and the three of us broke down and cried—so much so that the bridal shop insisted I take it off before I washed it with mascara.

And speaking of which, Mom and Sam have already cried off their makeup twice to be exact—and after the third application, Myrna, the makeup artist, suggested they wait in the sanctuary with the rest of the guests. I figured it was costing her some serious inventory to keep reapplying all of those formidable layers that make both Sam and Mom look that much more like the beauties they are.

Savy breezes back into the room. "Auntie Missy, I've got a note! It's a love letter from Uncle Graham." My heart melts each time she calls him that. Holly thought it was best to start right away, and by New Year's Eve, Savy wouldn't call him anything else.

"A note!" I sing as Holly does a nervous dance between the door and me.

"There's no time for notes," my sister blurts. "Ruby says we're on in five."

I make a face. It's almost amusing the way Holly keeps referencing my wedding as if it were a musical. I peel back the envelope and pull out a beautiful card with a familiar picture on the front, and I catch my breath, my body already bucking with tears. It's the picture we took at the lake last Christmas—Graham, Noel, and me with our lopsided snowman photo bombing us from behind.

I land my hand over my mouth as I read it.

Sprig,

Are you nervous yet? Don't be. In a few minutes, I'll be holding your hand and I'll continue to do so as your husband until my very last breath. Today is the happiest day of my life, and I plan on drinking down every single moment. I already know you will glow like a shining star as you make your way down that aisle. Just know that I already have tears in my eyes at the thought of seeing you. I have a smile on my face knowing that I'll get to kiss you before too long. And I have hope in my heart that our future will bring us much love and laughter. I know it will. It's inevitable, just like we were all along.

All of my heart forever,

Graham

Holly sobs from over my shoulder. "Oh, for Pete's sake! *Myrna!*"

And just like that, Myrna pulls off a mascara miracle for both Holly and me.

Before long, Holly is gone, and I watch as Savy holds Noel by the leash as they ready to head in after her mother.

"Savy," I whisper, hoping that Ruby won't hear. She's a bit high-strung and has warned me that Italian lace and yellow labs that have a propensity to hug you are not a match made in bridal heaven. "Bring Noel over." I wrinkle my nose as I give a quick look around.

There aren't any windows into the sanctuary, so I can't even get a glimpse of how handsome Graham must be. I already know he is. It's a given.

Savanah swishes over in her petal pink dress, a rhinestone encrusted tiara pressed over her head. "I won't tell," she whispers back. "Go ahead and give her a hug."

And I bend over and do just that. "Hey, you?" I try to fight the tears, and she licks my cheek. "You're the reason Mommy and Daddy are together, you know that? I love you so much. You be a good girl today, okay? We'll play again later, I promise." I stand and flatten my hands over the front of my dress.

Savy pulls Noel a safe distance away. "You should really look into getting her a brother or a sister."

"Right." I avert my eyes at the thought. "I can hardly handle one puppy, let alone two."

"Not even a *human* puppy?" Her violet-colored Winters

women's eyes widen with glee. As much as I appreciate Tom, I'm glad Savy's genetics swayed toward the Winters' gene pool.

"A human puppy?" A quick chuckle bounces from my chest. "You mean a baby?" I whisper so low it sounds like a secret.

"Yes"—she nods heavily as if she couldn't annunciate it enough—"a *baby*. Plus, that way, I'll have a real live doll to play with."

The frazzled wedding coordinator pops up, and she sheds a soothing crimson smile. "You're up, girls."

"Oh my goodness." Suddenly I can't breathe or think or move.

The bridal march begins, and all of my senses suddenly feel heightened, and tears spontaneously blur my vision. My body goes numb, and my feet move just the way they're supposed to as I follow Savy and Noel to the entry of the church only to find every pew filled to capacity, and each and every body standing at attention, looking this way. A fiery panic rips through me, and the sudden urge to bolt and avoid all this attention hits me. But my eyes follow that white runner right down the aisle until my gaze lands on a tall, dark, and devilishly handsome Graham Holiday.

Dad comes in close and threads his arm through mine, offers a kiss to my cheek, and we start down the aisle. I don't dare take my eyes off that handsome man waiting for me with a wide smile, tear-filled eyes. And when Savy and Noel do something so cute it has the entire congregation giggling, I totally miss it. I can't seem to take my eyes off my future husband. Don't want to.

My father lands me safely next to Graham, kisses my cheek once again, and this time the tears glide down my face.

The ceremony moves quickly, and before I know it, it's time for Graham and me to read our vows to one another.

I nod a quick thank you as Holly hands me my notes.

"You're going to kill it!" she whispers before jumping back to her post.

I look up into my precious fiancé's bright blue eyes and get lost for a brief moment in the tranquility they exude. A part of me wishes we would have saved the vows for later when we were alone. But then I'm pretty sure we'll be a bit busy once we're behind closed doors. A naughty smile curves on my lips, and his left brow rises with his amusement.

"Graham"—my voice breaks, and I do my best to clear my throat—"it seems I have known you all of my life. And for as long as I can remember, I have looked forward to seeing you. Just having you near me was as soothing as it was annoying at times." A gentle laugh fills the room. "And once you came back to Gingerbread, I knew instantly I felt something for you, something new that I didn't quite know what to do with." I glance to the crowd. "I guess most of you are familiar with that story." A rumble of laughter circulates once again. I look back to Graham and hook my eyes to his. There's something spellbinding about the moment, and a part of me wants to hit the pause button on the festivities. "But I want you to know that I do know what to do with you from this point forward. I'm going to love you. I'm going to support your hopes and dreams. I'm going to be there for you through the highs and lows, and I'm going to listen when you need me to listen. I look forward to starting and ending each and every day with you for the rest of our lives. I'm the luckiest girl in the world. Thank you for choosing me."

Graham's entire body shakes and trembles as he struggles to keep it together, and suddenly it feels like an impossible feat for both of us.

The minister nods to Graham, and he quickly wipes down his tears.

"Missy"—he swallows hard as if it were taking all his strength to do this—"you have always been my favorite person to torment." The room lights up with a laugh and so do I. "And, now, I'm going to spend the rest of my life making it up to you. There's not a day that will go by without me expressing my heartfelt love to you. I've been all over the world looking for something—what, I wasn't quite sure. I thought New York might finally hold the answer, and yet it wasn't until I came back to Gingerbread, back to *you*, that I found it. What I needed most was right here at home all along. I'm thankful that we finally made our way to one another." He takes up both my hands, and my entire body relaxes for the first time since I set foot in this church. "Mistletoe, I promise to love and honor you all the days of our lives. I'm going to cherish you, cherish each moment we get to spend together as husband and wife. Life is an adventure, and I'm glad you chose to have this adventure with me."

The minister ushers the ceremony along. We light the unity candle and join hands once again. He says a little prayer over the two of us, so beautiful my eyes sting with tears once again.

He nods to Graham. "You may now kiss your bride."

I can't help but smile as Graham leans in and lands a precious kiss right over my lips and lingers.

The minister clears his throat, and the crowd breaks out into applause and laughter.

"Ladies and gentlemen, for the first time ever, let me introduce you to Mr. and Mrs. Graham Holiday!"

The crowd goes wild, and Noel breaks free from Savanah's hold and leaps and barks with glee, right along with everyone else. Graham takes me by the hand, and we race down the aisle with Noel racing by our side.

We hit the foyer, and Graham leads us out through the open doors where the sunshine warms our backs.

Graham takes up both my hands and sheds a smile as wide as the sea. "We did it, Sprig."

"We did indeed. You ready for what comes next?"

"As long as you're by my side, I think we've got it all."

We share another kiss as the bodies stream from the church to offer their congratulations.

Graham is right.

As long as we're together, we really do have it all.

Mrs. Graham Holiday, I marvel to myself. With Graham in my life, as my husband, every day will feel like Christmas.

Graham

Nine months later...

There are nights where I have marveled at how beautiful my wife is, but tonight at the annual community center auction, on this snowy Christmas Eve, she simply takes my breath away.

"Merry Christmas." Tanner pops up and slaps me over the shoulder.

"Merry Christmas," I parrot right back as Missy makes her way over in a stunning red dress. Her hands cradle her beautiful belly, and I love her that much more knowing she's cradling our child safely in her arms. She's due any minute now. I offered to sit this one out with her, but Missy wouldn't hear of it. She's never missed a Christmas benefit yet, and she wasn't about to start now.

"Here they come." Tanner welcomes Sabrina Jarrett with open arms. This will mark one year that the two of them have been seeing one another. To be honest, I gave it a week, but Sabrina seems genuinely interested in Tanner, and I couldn't be happier for the two of them.

Missy joins our small circle and wraps her arms around my waist. "So, how's everything at Holiday Pies?" She looks to Tanner. "This one won't take me out to Cater to check on the factory. He's too afraid to be five minutes away from the hospital."

Sabrina grimaces at my beautiful wife. "Can't blame him. Face it, you look ready to pop!"

Missy glances up at her with that impatient look in her eye. "I am ready to pop. I can't believe I was hardly able to help at the bakery for the last six weeks."

"Doctor's orders." I lift my hands as if surrendering. "I had nothing to do with it."

Tanner leans in. "Plus, you're still settling in from the move. That nursery you set up with a view of the lake? Sign me up to babysit. I can get used to looking out that window all day long."

The four of us share a laugh. Mom and Dad come over, along with Joy and Jack. I feel as if the Winters are every bit family, and oddly I've always regarded them that way.

Joy gives a playful snarl over at her daughter. "When are you going to have that sweet angel so I can kiss and squeeze those baby cheeks?"

Mom offers an aggressive nod. "And I'm dying to know if it's a girl or a boy. I just can't stand not knowing."

Dad tucks his elbow to her arm. "She's tired of knitting everything yellow."

"I like yellow," Missy offers. She's been more than kind enough to go along with all of my mother's schemes and baby dreams. Mom and Joy threw us a baby shower at the house, and the entire theme was gray elephants. Missy didn't say an unkind word, but once we were alone, she wondered if her size had inadvertently inspired it. I assured her that it had nothing to do with it. Missy looks perfect to me in any size.

Holly and Tom come up, along with Savanah. And Holly wrinkles her nose at her sister. "Are you still holding in that baby? How about giving us all a nice little gift and pushing that puppy out for all to see?"

Savanah's little face lights up. "I knew you were having a puppy!" She takes off screaming, "*She's having a puppy! She's having a puppy!*" And the entire lot of us breaks out into laughter.

Nick comes over and slaps me over the shoulder. "We did it. Another year at the tree lot under our belt."

"That's right, man" I pull him in and land an arm over his shoulder. "And I'm helping you out next year, too." I pull Missy in with my other arm. "And we should have one more helper to add to the staff."

"Ow!" Missy shouts, and I lift my arm off her shoulder.

"Sorry about that."

"You didn't do it." Her forehead wrinkles with worry as she winces hard. "It's the baby. I've been feeling contractions all day, and they've just been getting worse and worse."

"*What?*" Holly jumps forward and lands her hands gently over Missy's burgeoning belly. "Why didn't you tell me?"

"I didn't want to ruin anyone's Christmas. It's probably nothing." Missy tips her head back and lets out a harrowing cry, altering us to the fact it's definitely something.

And just like that, sheer chaos ensues. Our parents mobilize in every direction at once. Tanner and Sabrina appear and do their best to run me out the door. Our entire motley crew ambles out to the parking lot, and an entire fleet of cars attempts to speed out of the lot at once. I jump into the truck and do my best to speed around them.

"Hang on, Missy." I glance her way and note the seat is empty. "*Missy!*" I hit the brakes and spot her standing alone at the entry and throw the truck in reverse. "I'm so sorry!" I rush out and help her into the passenger's seat, carefully buckling her in, and wave as if I were seeing her off.

"What are you doing?" she howls into the night.

"I don't know!" I shout as I hop back into the truck and speed us all the way to the hospital. Missy and I are about to take that next step—have a baby, become parents.

Life is about to change in a spectacular way.

I just hope I don't pass out and miss it.

Six hours later, after much labored breathing, much coaching from Holly and me, and a heck of a lot of work from

Missy herself—the staff has left us alone with our very own pink bundle of joy.

I land a sweet kiss to our new daughter's rosy cheek and then to my wife's as I sit on the edge of Missy's hospital bed. "Merry Christmas to my two favorite girls—and to the one we've got at home, too."

"That's right!" Missy's face lights up. In truth, she hasn't stopped glowing for the last nine months. "Noel has a brand new baby sister." She curls her finger over the baby's precious chin. "You know, we have to give her a name."

A dull moan comes from me. Missy and I have hit a dead end each time we've tried to come up with something. "Now that she's here, I'm sure we'll figure it out pretty quickly. I mean, she looks like she could be a—" I pause because I have no clue where I'm going with this. Her cute button nose and sleepy eyes have already wrapped themselves around my heart. And that shock of dark hair made Missy coo with delight as soon as she saw it.

Missy takes a deep breath. "She was born on Christmas. How about something holiday related?" She looks up at me.

"Holiday Holiday." We both shake our heads, shooting down my idea at once. "I don't know. What about days of the week or months or birthstones?"

"Well, it's Tuesday. That's cute, but it just doesn't fit. It is December?" She shrugs up at me, and both our eyes light up at once. "*December*," she coos down at the sleeping angel in her arms. "We can call her Ember for short. I love that so much, do you?" Tears swell in her eyes as she looks to me, and I nod.

"December it is."

"And we know the middle name." Missy reaches over and pulls my arm around her and the baby. Missy and I decided firmly that whatever gender our child would be, we would give him or her our parents' first names as their middle name. Her mother's if it was a girl, and my father's if it was a boy. And with our next child, we'll do the same. Missy and I plan on having quite the brood, at least three, but Missy insists it's more like four. "December Joy Holiday."

"That sounds just perfect. I love you, Missy. And I love you, sweet December."

A gentle knock comes over the door as Holly peeks her head in, and soon the room is filled with our loved ones all gathered around to marvel at our tiny bundle of December joy. One by one, they congratulate us, and the love brimming in this room makes it feel like Christmas.

Missy and I hold our baby tight long into the night.

Missy looks to me with sleepy eyes as the sun breaks free on this Christmas morning. "How are we ever going to top this next year?"

I give a light chuckle. "I guess we'll have to have twins."

Missy's mouth falls open. "You do realize that the first wish you make on Christmas morning will inevitably come true."

"So, you're saying I should have asked for triplets?"

She looks as if she'd like to swat me, but she's too exhausted to execute the idea.

"I guess that means we'll be growing our brood faster than we thought." She bites down on a smile.

"I couldn't think of a better person to do just that with."

"Me either. Merry Christmas, Graham."

"Merry Christmas, Missy."

And just like that, we arrive at our happily ever after with no end to the joy in sight. Just the way we like it.

I knew something was missing in my life right up until I set foot back in Gingerbread.

It turns out, all I needed was a little Mistletoe.

Acknowledgements

Thank you to YOU, the reader, for sharing in this Christmas adventure with me. There is nothing like the joy of the holidays, and I hope this book brought you a taste of it.

Special thanks to Jodie Tarleton for gracing this book with your beautiful eyes. How can I ever convey how thankful I am for you? You are truly a treasure.

To the fabulous Kaila Eileen Turingan-Ramos who is a ninja in her own right. You are fierce in every capacity. Thank you for sharing your wisdom with me!

Thank you to the sweet Shay Rivera, best beta ever! I hope every day of your life is merry and bright.

A hearty thanks to Lisa Markson. Every day is Christmas with you in my life. I love you.

To the queen of all words, Paige Maroney Smith, I'm always thankful to have my books in your presence. You are the greatest gift!

And last, but never least, thank you to Him who sits on the throne. Worthy is the Lamb! Glory and honor and power are yours. I owe you everything.

About the Author

Addison Moore is a **New York Times**, **USA Today**, and **Wall Street Journal** bestselling author who writes contemporary and paranormal romance. Her work has been featured in **Cosmopolitan** Magazine. Previously she worked as a therapist on a locked psychiatric unit for nearly a decade. She resides on the West Coast with her husband, four wonderful children, and two dogs where she eats too much chocolate and stays up way too late. When she's not writing, she's reading.

Feel free to visit her at:

Website: www.addisonmoore.com
Facebook: Addison Moore Author
Twitter: @AddisonMoore
Instagram: @AuthorAddisonMoore
http://addisonmoorewrites.blogspot.com